A Nick Bancroft Mystery
MURDER BY THE BOOK

Bob Liter

Bob Liter

and daughter
Martie Liter Ogborn

Digital Parchment Press

BOB LITER'S
Nick Bancroft Mysteries

CONTENTS

INTRODUCTION

Welcome to *Murder by the Book,* the first novel in the series of Nick Bancroft Mysteries. While reading my Dad's books, preparing them for re-release, I discovered how much of himself he put into the stories. I hope you enjoy the puzzling who-done-it and the fascinating character study of Bob Liter aka Nick Bancroft who, by some standards, is just a good man who falls into the strangest situations.

For a proper introduction, here is a brief history and a few revealing stories of Robert T "Bob" Liter. (1923-2008) Dad was born in Iowa to Charles and Hazel Liter. The only boy in a family with two sisters, Bob was enterprising and caddied at the Des Moines neighborhood golf course where a golf-pro took Dad under his wing and taught him the game of golf. Although Bob was a lefty, left-handed golf clubs were hard to come by, so the golf-pro taught him how to play with a right-handed set. Bob learned and mastered many sports left-handed, although all his life he played golf right-handed and never forgot the generosity of his first golf instructor.

Shortly after high school, Bob enlisted. As a Navy seaman recruit in World War II, one of his early assignments was a water boiler operator on a Landing Ship, Tank (LST) to support military amphibious operations. Along with other irreverent sailors who manned these curious ships, they sarcastically claimed the acronym stood for "Large Slow Target." Hope, courage, and persistence went a long way during his years in the Navy.

One story I remember hearing, Dad was on shore leave in North Africa with fellow crew members all dressed in sailor whites for a night on the town. Returning to the ship, slightly inebriated, the group wandered through an oil field. Their shoes were covered in black muck. In the morning it was apparent that Bob would be in trouble. His small shoe size, a men's 5, and the small footprints on the deck leading to his bunk easily convicted Seaman Recruit Liter. Bob was the only one to serve time in The Brig for the indiscretion.

Between his tours of duty, World War II and the Korean War, Bob attended and graduated from Drake University, School of Journalism and married my Mom.

Lillian Hyde, soon to be Lillian Liter, had graduated from high school and was working at S.S. Kresge's new FIVE and DIME in Des Moines. She would regularly be impressed by a cocky young fella named Bob who would come by the store and visit while she worked. She could always tell when he was near, because from three aisles away she could hear the taps on his shoes and the tunes he would whistle as he walked toward her.

Bob Liter and Lillian Hyde were married on March 4, 1950 and honeymooned. It must have been some honeymoon, because not long after the wedding, Mom tells the story of sitting on a park bench in the quad of Mount Mercy University in Cedar Rapids, Iowa close to their apartment and telling Dad I was on the way. I was born in November of 1950 around Thanksgiving. My Dad named me Martie Lynn. Mom and I didn't find out until years later he had named me after a waitress he had a crush on while he was in the service.

Dad's hope, courage, and persistence proved to be stepping stones into the newspaper world. Our family now included my sister and brother. The family moved to Lincoln, IL and Bob went to work at the Lincoln Courier. Dad had the opportunity to pass along the generosity of his first golf instructor to John Swingle. Here is the story in John's own words:

"A week after I received my high school diploma I received a call from my hometown newspaper. I think it was the next day I had an interview with Bob Liter, city editor, about a summer proofreading job. Little did I know that Bob Liter was about to become my boss, my mentor, a terrific friend, confidant, and an exceptional influence on the rest of my life! He welcomed me to meet his family, a relationship which continues to this day. Bob Liter was a terrific teacher that passed along his knowledge of the newspaper business on a practical everyday basis and not classroom programs. With that knowledge I launched my newspaper career that I enjoyed all of my working days. Bob Liter was a true newspaperman with a talent for writing, and an exceptional friend! My sincere thanks, Bob!"

MARTIE LITER OGBORN

CHAPTER ONE

Tires screeched as I started across Commerce Street on my way to Otto's Tavern for breakfast. I jumped back to the curb. Half a block to my left a battered pickup truck swerved around a man running in the middle of the street. Damn. It was Broadway John. His canvas shoes slapped the hot, cracked pavement with each uneven stride. The truck, loaded with junk for the scrap yard, rattled by.

Broadway John pulled up gasping for air.

"Mister, I think she's dead. She lost her clothes, and she's like a stiff dog I found once," he said.

"What do you mean, 'she's dead?' Who?"

"She's all stiff and cold, like the dog."

"Who?"

"I don't know."

"All right, just calm down."

"She's at the football stadium, sitting in the first row. Doubled up with a book in her lap. You know, Centrel High, up on the bluff. I was looking for cans."

He carried his usual plastic garbage bag. It was empty. I ignored the lack of logic in looking for aluminum cans in August at a football stadium. I didn't want to get involved, damn it. I didn't want to hurt his feelings either.

"Come on," I said. "We'll drive up there."

I retrieved my ancient Escort from behind the nearly abandoned office building I had just left. The car sputtered the ten blocks or so to the stadium. We parked at the gate beside a police patrol car. Broadway John, or BJ as I called him, was trying to force a pair of thick eyeglasses onto his face.

"Look what I found," he said proudly, holding them toward me.

"Don't try to wear them. They're too small. They'll give you a headache. Come on."

The football field was surrounded by link fence, but the gate was open. We crossed the cinder track and headed toward the wooden bleachers on the grassy field. BJ trotted ahead. A policeman standing on the cinder track stopped him. Crime-scene

1

tape was stretched from the top of the bleachers to a stake driven into the track and then back to the top.

When I caught up BJ insisted, "She was right there, right there." He pointed to the front row of the stands near the 50-yard line. Tears joined perspiration on his face.

"I believe you BJ. Police must have taken the body away. Let's go back to the car."

"What does he know about this?" the cop, a young patrolman I didn't know, asked. "There was a body. Homicide has been here and left. The body was taken to the morgue."

I explained that BJ saw the body when he was looking for aluminum cans.

"I'll give Detective Andy Brown all the details, but I want to get BJ out of here, okay?" The cop took our names and reluctantly allowed us to leave.

BJ still was confused about what happened to the body. I changed the subject.

"Don't look for cans at the football stadium in the summer. You'll find more in Hellerman Park. Don't stay around there too long, either. Remember, I told you to stay away from there when the bad guys come."

By the time we got to Hellerman Park, a block-square playground taken over at night by drug dealers, he was humming a tune I couldn't quite place. I left him there and returned to what I had started to do, get breakfast at the tavern. I told BJ's story to Otto Kamp, the bar owner, as I gnawed on a doughnut almost as stale as the air in the place.

"I suppose you want another cup of coffee," Otto said. I nodded. He added another figure to my tab.

"You better call Brown."

"Yeah, I guess I should."

I called Detective Andrew Brown, Centrel City, Illinois' finest, and explained how BJ found the body and how police already had taken it to the morgue when I returned BJ to the scene. Brown said a woman who runs every morning there called in.

"She must have been there right after BJ. I don't suppose it will help to talk to him but bring him in just in case," Andy said.

I agreed and figured that would be the end of my involvement. Sure, and I'd also win the lottery.

The next morning I sat at Otto's bar reading the sports pages of the Centrel City Press. Otto sat in a worn, cushioned chair behind the bar. A wall lamp cast shadows beyond his ancient head. He commented from time to time on the news in the front section of the newspaper. I was trying not to listen. I was perturbed because there was no report on the Professional Bowlers' Association national tournament in Milwaukee. The finals were to be on television the next Saturday. It pissed me off that the paper had room for local dart ball results but no room for a national bowling tournament.

It was around 10 o'clock. The sun partially penetrated the dirt on the front windows. I know because I was looking in that direction, composing in my mind the blistering letter to the newspaper I would never write, when a man I later learned was Ramsey Sinclair, opened the front door, hesitated, allowing sunlight to actually enter the place, and said in a voice that carried to every corner, "Is Nick Bancroft here?"

That's me. I couldn't see much against the light, but I noted the classy cut of his suit and decided it looked too expensive to be owned by a bill collector.

Still, I hesitated to answer. He said, "Well, surely the question is not that difficult for you two ... gentlemen."

"I'm Nick Bancroft," I said.

"Could I tear you away from all this and back to your office long enough to discuss business?"

I stiffened.

Otto must have noticed. He said, "Mister Bancroft was just saying it's time for him to get back to work."

Sinclair turned and left. I followed in the wake of his long strides as we crossed the street, went up the creaking wooden stairs, past the Ballard Inc. office on the second floor and up to the third floor.

The notice from my office door informing potential customers I could be found at Otto's was on the floor. A dirty, chipped blue bowl near the note reminded me I forgot to feed the cat.

My office consisted of a worn, oversized wooden desk with drawers that stuck, a swivel chair that didn't always swivel, and some battered filing cabinets. In front of the desk was a wooden chair for the occasional visitor. A radio with a cracked plastic case sat on the window ledge beside an ancient air-conditioner. The window overlooked the parking lot in back of the building. A one-room apartment adjoined the office. The rest of the third floor housed cobwebs and dust.

I settled behind the desk. Sinclair rejected my offer to sit after looking at the "guest" chair. He was slender and a shade over six feet tall. His hair and eyebrows were black. Touches of silver highlighted his sideburns. His close set, penetrating eyes glared at me. His thin lips were turned down, reminding me of a drama mask.

He asked me to investigate the murder of his daughter, Linsley. "I'm sure you know about it by now. Her body was found at the football stadium. I'm from Chicago, but I used to live in this burg years ago, and I have contacts here. I'm told you're the person most likely to find out who killed my daughter."

I said, "First you should know, just for the record, that I am not a licensed private investigator. I'm an ex-reporter who inherited this sorry office from a friend for whom I occasionally worked. He died and had the bad taste to leave me his dying detective agency. It offered me a chance to live here for awhile and quit the entertainment business that passes as news."

Sinclair didn't need to know the place was rent free for a few more months because my benefactor had paid it in advance, and that I was just drifting until the rent ran out.

He informed me he knew all the details about my squalid existence – he didn't actually say squalid, just implied it – and said he wanted an answer.

I said, "Yes."

"I'll pay you two-hundred dollars a day. I expect a telephone report tomorrow at four o'clock. Four o'clock. Don't make me wait. I'll deduct from your pay for every second I wait for your call."

He handed me an envelope and left. It contained ten one-hundred dollar bills and a card bearing his name and phone number.

I stuffed the money into my billfold and took a can of cat food from the filing cabinet, opened the thing, and put the stuff in the bowl. My cat responsibilities were met for another day. I went across the street to Otto's and my favorite stool.

"Now tell me again how much I owe you, Mister Bartender," I said.

"I suppose you want another cup of coffee."

I fanned the bills near his face.

"Here's a hundred, my man. It was twenty-six dollars for coffee and those things you call doughnuts and seventy-three for beer, right? You may not keep the change. However, get yourself a beer on me, and I'll have one also."

Otto stared at the money. "It's too early for beer for you ... or me. That guy hire you to rob a bank? Pay you in advance? Thanks for taking care of me before you pay the others."

"You and the office utilities – those are the ones I pay first."

He put the money in his billfold, took a dollar out of the cash register, and handed it to me. He tore up the tab that had been next to the cash register for several weeks.

He placed a cup of coffee in front of me. "On the house," he said.

"Sure, now that I have money you offer free coffee. When I'm broke you charge it to my account. Great."

Otto turned to his chair behind the bar, sighed, and sat down. He was at least 60 years old, judging from his wrinkled face, although we never discussed his age. He probably weighed 200 pounds even though he was little more than five feet tall. He wore baggy pants, a pair of squashed shoes, and T-shirts that advertised things. For some reason I liked the guy. Maybe he was a father image.

I told him about the case. He got up and riffled through newspapers on a small table near his chair. "Ya, here it is." He handed me the newspaper section containing the report on the death of Linsley Sinclair. The paper identified her as a 33-year-old resident of Centrel City. Cause of death, according to the report, still was under investigation.

Detective Andrew Brown was quoted, but, as usual, he didn't offer much. Brown and I had argued many times about his withholding information that, according to me, belonged to the public.

"Wow," Otto said. "You're in the big league at last. I may never have to loan you beer money again."

"Yes, but I may not be big league long. Sinclair didn't give me a chance to explain that I probably can't find out more than the police. Brown is on the case, and he's good."

"You solved the Anderson case when you were a reporter. Why not this one?"

"Yeah, why not," I said as I slid from the bar stool and left.

The sun did a job on my eyes before they adjusted, otherwise I might have avoided BJ. Still, I had promised to get him to the police station. The poor guy thinks I'm the greatest thing since the last Broadway musical because I did a piece on him a couple of years ago when I still worked for a living. He's been a character around the downtown area for more years than anyone could remember. He's big, bony, has a hawk nose, but has the mind of a child – a sweet, harmless child.

He knew a bushel of Broadway songs from musicals and usually sang at least one whenever we met. His real name was John Snyder. He walked with me and sang to himself, lost in his own musical world. Apparently he had forgotten about the body.

We walked by a pool hall, a couple of taverns as forlorn as Otto's, Lou's Restaurant, and several boarded up businesses to get to the police station three blocks away.

The cement steps leading to the station were worn from constant traffic over the years. I climbed them once again.

"Hey, where you been?" asked the desk sergeant, a guy named Morris, as we entered the main room with its high ceiling, soiled windows, and scattered desks.

The ringing of telephones, the hum of conversation, occasional shouting, and the long counter designed to keep the public at bay reminded me that maybe I missed the place. I had spent a lot of time there as a reporter.

Morris gave me the prepared-for-the-media reports on Linsley Sinclair's murder. I leaned against the counter as I read them and wrote in a small notebook. He gave me a questioning look as BJ continued his singsong routine. When I finished BJ and I went around the counter to Brown's office. Brown talked to him briefly.

"What a witness he would make," Brown said after BJ left when I told him we had private business. I invited Brown for a cup of coffee at the Lucky Diner across the street. It has been there forever and probably never passed a health department test, but at least it was convenient. After we got the coffee I informed Andy that Ramsey Sinclair had hired me to find out who killed his daughter.

Andy, who is about my height and weight, five feet ten and 180 pounds, and about my age, late thirties, put his left hand on top of his bald head and said, "Why in the world would he hire a broken down bowler to investigate anything?"

"He's heard how good I am, I suppose."

"How good you are? The lawyers seem to think you're capable of investigating traffic accidents. Desperate people sometimes hire you to gather divorce evidence, but a murder?"

Andy, with his angry dark eyes and jutting chin, intimidated witnesses. He also intimidated most reporters and other low types. However I had learned to get past his tough exterior and was no longer awed by him.

"I read all the police reports. Tell me what the reports don't say."

It annoyed me, the need to beg for information from "public servants." It was no different when I questioned Andy, although he was less arrogant and self-serving than most.

"How much is this guy paying you to tell him what police have found out so far?" Andy asked.

6

"Enough so I don't mind buying you coffee. He demanded that I give him a report by tomorrow afternoon. You always know more than you tell reporters. Give me a break. If this story is good enough I'll sell it to one of the Chicago papers. I can make you a hero."

"Would you do that for me? Gee, wouldn't that be swell." He leaned toward me. "The victim's mother lives here. She's in the phone book. Mrs. Ramsey Sinclair. She's divorced. Never remarried. And there is this thing that you must promise to keep quiet, at least for now."

I nodded. I had almost always kept promises I made to him. An overhead fan groaned as it pushed hot air our way. The skinny, redheaded waitress behind the counter laughed as she talked to a customer. I waited.

"There were no marks on the body except a small one on the left arm, like a pin prick. The lab people probably will find that something lethal was injected into her system. And whoever killed her put a sex etiquette book on her lap."

A sex etiquette book. No wonder he had kept it quiet so far. The media would have a ball with that.

"Anything you find out you give me, right?"

I agreed. Before it was over he held out on me and I returned the favor.

CHAPTER TWO

Mrs. Ramsey Sinclair answered when I phoned. She refused to be interviewed until I mentioned her ex-husband had hired me.

"That snake. You mean he's parting with some of his precious money? He never paid much attention to Linsley when she was alive."

"Nobody gets away with murdering my daughter," he told me when he hired me.

"That would be his attitude. It's not about her. If it will help find out what happened I'll answer all the questions again," she said.

She agreed to an interview that afternoon. I had time to get my car and buy a full tank of gas. I even had the oil changed.

The ungrateful car still sputtered and resisted idling as I drove away from lower Centrel City's ancient clutter into cleaner air and surroundings. Mrs. Sinclair's house was five blocks from Centrel City High School and the football stadium where her daughter's body was found.

The house was one of many look-a-likes in a middle class neighborhood. A two-seat swing hung from the ceiling of the front porch, and a large pot of red geraniums sat to the side of the top step. As I climbed the steps Mrs. Sinclair opened the door and invited me in. She appeared older than her ex-husband but then her hair wasn't dyed black. However, she was trim, like a woman who does the physical stuff. Her eyes, whatever their natural color, were bleary red.

It was cool and dark inside the house. As my eyes adjusted a couple of stuffed chairs, a couch a man could nap on, and dark, worn carpeting, came into view.

I apologized for the questions. She recited Linsley Sinclair's history to the point I interrupted to get her back near the present.

Linsley, according to her, had been living in her old room upstairs.

"She never married?" I asked.

"Oh, she could have, yes, she could. She had plenty of offers, but she just wasn't interested. I never understood why."

8

I followed Mrs. Sinclair up a stairway to the second floor. Linsley's room was home to several stuffed animals, a couple of large dolls, and ruffled curtains that matched the red and white gingham bedspread. I didn't see anything significant until I found her high school yearbook on the top shelf of the closet. It smelled of stale perfume. Mrs. Sinclair agreed to let me take the book after I promised to return it.

She looked at it and sobbed. She sat on the bed and held a rag doll with a clownish smile on its faded face. "Linsley stayed out late much of the time after she moved back from Chicago where she had lived with her father. She would not say where she had been or with whom," Mrs. Sinclair said.

"I'm not your little girl any more," she quoted Linsley as saying, making it sound as caustic as Ramsey Sinclair.

"How much time did she spend with her father?"

Mrs. Sinclair dabbed at her eyes with a lace handkerchief and sighed.

"She spent part of several summers up in Chicago. I imagine she was left alone much of the time. By the time she was in high school she had become as much of a snob as him. I tried to overcome his influence, but I failed."

"Do you have any idea who might have killed her?"

"No. Why would anyone want to kill Lins?"

When I left Mrs. Sinclair still was dabbing at her eyes. She accepted my condolences and apologized for crying.

A nice woman. Such a contrast to her abrasive ex-husband. After parking the car behind my office, I climbed those damned stairs and waved at Maggie Atley from the hall as I went by the Ballard Inc. office. She was the friendly receptionist who reminded me with her daily greetings that there were other things in life besides beer and bowling.

She and I shared the responsibility of feeding the cat. In my office I checked to see if there were any phone messages. It was no surprise to find none.

I sat around for a few minutes thinking about the case and waiting for four o'clock so I could go across the street for a beer. The four o'clock bit was Otto's rule for himself and somehow had become mine ... most of the time.

On the second floor, as I headed down to the street, Maggie waved from her desk.

"How you doing?" she asked.

I went into the office and handed her the high school yearbook I was carrying. She looked at it, then at me. I leaned over the desk, took her face in my hands, tilted it to mine, and kissed her long and tender on those sweeter-than-wine lips.

"That's how I'm doing," I said. "Drop over to Otto's after you get off, and I'll buy you a drink."

I took the yearbook from her nail-polished fingers and left before she could speak, carrying the pleasant memory of the astonished look in her wondrous blue eyes and the intoxicating smell of her. *If I ever again get serious about a woman...* I tossed the thought aside like an unpaid bill. I bounced down the rest of the stairs and out the door. I got a glass of beer, bought Otto one, and retired to a back booth to read the yearbook.

Since the body was found at the football field I figured maybe her high school past had something to do with the reason why she was murdered.

Linsley Sinclair apparently wasn't active in after-school clubs or much of anything else connected to the school. Her photo showed a sharp-featured, carefully made up face. She had blonde hair and pale blue eyes, attractive in a brittle way. In the photo she looked down her nose at the photographer, and perhaps the world. I went through the yearbook page by page. My beer was warm by the time I finished. I had learned Linsley was one-quarter of the "grand quartet."

The group included Harold Hubbard, son of the owner of the largest furniture store in Centrel City, Charlie Connor, the high school's Allstate football halfback, and Laura Beckert, daughter of Robert Beckert, Centrel City's mayor at the time.

I sipped beer and wondered what had happened by now to all the people behind the eager young faces. One, in particular, had grabbed my attention. I turned the pages back to the photograph of a kid named Rudolph Sluppleman.

His dark hair was cut short. His eyes were small and dark. They looked familiar. Did I know him?

He was quoted as saying his ambition was "to become a psychiatrist and learn why people are so inhumane."

Thoughts of the yearbook and the murder vanished when Maggie came in. I had offered to buy her a drink before, but she never showed. Now here she was, bringing light and a smile into the gloom of Otto's Tavern. She was wearing a wrinkle-free white dress with light blue stripes that accented her womanly accouterments. White sandals revealed manicured toes and highlighted tanned, slender ankles and legs. She was as pretty and fresh as a cold beer on a hot day. She smiled as I gazed at her, did a wisp of a curtsy, and sat down. I went to the bar and fetched the cola she wanted and got myself another beer. I ignored Otto's clucking as he served me.

"I'm surprised," I said. "What made you accept my offer this time?"

"Morbid curiosity overcame my fear of being seen in such a seedy place. It isn't as bad as I imagined. There is an unpleasant odor though."

"Just stale beer and stale bodies," I said. "A person can get used to it."

"I hope not," she said. "I'm intrigued about why you kissed me and why you're so happy. I suppose it has something to do with money. Did you win a bowling tournament?"

I told her about the case.

"But that had nothing to do with me kissing you. The kiss was pure impulse brought on by your enticing beauty."

"Of course," she said. She fluttered her eyelashes.

I started thinking of clever things I could say to impress her and was, at the same time, trying to halt the attempt. I didn't want to get involved, although...

She sipped at the cola until half the glass was empty and said she had to go. My plea for her to stay failed. I escorted her across the street to the parking lot behind our building. She thanked me for the drink. I bowed as she got into her Honda and asked if there was anything else I could do for her.

"Yes," she said. "Shave more often and press your clothes."

She smiled, displaying even white teeth. Her eyes sparkled like a kid's who had just told a joke. I thanked her silently for the words as she drove away. It was a strong reminder of one of the reasons why I was single. She may have thought she was joking, but I didn't think so.

As I headed back to Otto's I heard a commotion coming from an alley half a block from the tavern. I recognized BJ's voice as he cried, "Why you guys mad at me? I didn't do nothin'."

Three young punks, two of them big, were swinging and kicking at poor old BJ. He was ducking and swinging himself. Still, the punks were only playing. If they had been serious, I figured he'd be down by now. Just the other day an old guy had been beaten to death. I wondered if it started this way.

My impulse was to holler for help. Anger won out. I stood into the middle of the entrance to the dead-end alley, about ten yards from BJ and the punks, and said as quietly as I could, "What the hell's going on."

The only sound – besides my thumping heart – was the rustle

of newspaper pages as a breeze nudged them farther into the dead-end alley.

The attackers turned, glared, and swaggered toward me. The biggest one, over six feet tall and dressed in the ridiculously baggy and oversized clothes that were the rage of the moment among teenagers, grinned, revealing black holes where teeth were missing. He said, "Now isn't this the shits. A hero come to save Broadway John from the evil knights."

One, maybe two of them I could handle – but three? Fear gnawed at my guts as I held my ground.

"You must be brave knights," I said. "Do you get your kicks out of beating up old men?"

They stopped, now only a couple of yards from me. The biggest one said, "We ain't beating nobody. He's only been pushed a little. The old fart called us garbage. Nobody calls us garbage."

Silence. BJ leaned against a wall dabbing at his bleeding nose.

"Can't you guys find something else to do? Why not use your energy to clean up places like this alley? It would be good for your self-image. You wouldn't feel like scum."

"Listen to that, Lump," big guy said, turning to the other two. "This guy must be my old man in disguise. My old man's always tellin' me what I should do while he sits around on his fat ass, drinks beer, and does nothin'. Never helps me or nobody."

"So you get a couple of other punks and go around beating up old people. That makes sense."

"Don't you call us punks. We can bust your nose too, you know," the biggest guy said.

"Sorry," I said. "I shouldn't have called you punks. You're knights, right? What's your name?"

They wouldn't tell me their names. I walked to BJ, expecting a blow to the head at any moment. I grasped his elbow and led him toward the street. He cringed as we passed the teenagers.

The big guy, behind us by then, shouted, "Well, Sir Galahad, how do we find you when we start cleaning up this alley? You and the old guy would want to help, wouldn't you?"

"The guy who owns Otto's Tavern always knows where I am," I replied as BJ limped along beside me.

He thanked me profusely as I took him to his basement room a couple of blocks away. I cleaned his bloody nose and left, promising I'd see him again soon.

"Stay away from those guys," was my parting advice.

"They find *me*, Mister," he said.

After going back to Otto's I sat at a booth and sipped beer. I worried about BJ as I tried to get my mind back on the investigation.

I found Harold Hubbard's home number in Otto's torn, dog-eared phone book. There also were numbers listed for three Hubbard furniture stores.

By then it was seven o'clock, and I thought he might be home. He wasn't, according to the woman who answered. I called the downtown store, the one his father founded, and was told he probably was at the west side store. He was.

"How may I help you?" was his question when we were connected. I introduced myself and explained I was investigating the murder of Linsley Sinclair. I requested an appointment so I could ask some routine questions.

"I've been all through that with police," he said. "They'll give you my answers, I suppose. I'm too busy to spend more time on this. Nick Bancroft? Do I know you?"

He did not sound impressed when I said he may have read the name from my newspaper exposure. I mentioned that Ramsey Sinclair, the murdered girl's father, had hired me.

"Ramsey Sinclair." He sounded like an awestruck employee talking about his boss. He asked for my telephone number and said he would call back. I gave him Otto's.

He called back in a few minutes and agreed to meet me first thing next morning at his downtown store.

CHAPTER THREE

The high school yearbook photo of Harold Hubbard showed a round face, shy smile, and curly brown hair. He was quoted as saying he was going to run away and join the circus after he graduated.

A snooty male clerk in the front of the store pointed to the back when I asked directions to Hubbard's office. I walked through a mile of stuffed chairs, cushy looking couches, and endless end tables on a carpet that sank with each step. The colors of the upholstered furniture ranged from outrageous to subdued. All suggested expensive.

At the back, near a glass-enclosed office with Venetian blinds, sat a small, elderly woman with straight hair dyed an outrageous shade of orange. The color failed to overshadow her bright eyes. She was surrounded by filing cabinets. Her desk was crowded by "in" and "out" baskets and a telephone. A name plate indicated she was "Millicent Hiller."

She agreed to allow me to enter Mister Hubbard's office "as long as he is expecting you."

In the office, doughnuts sat on the corner of a large polished desk along with a carafe of coffee. Behind the desk, in a chair that resembled a throne, sat Harold Hubbard. His hair had receded a couple of inches and no longer was curly. The shyness apparent in his high school photo was gone. He displayed a let's-get-down-to-business attitude. As I sat on the chrome-legged chair near the doughnuts and coffee, air hissed from the cushioned seat.

"I see you didn't join the circus," I said after he poured coffee.

He took a pencil out of a cup holding several and tapped it on the desk. He dropped it. "I don't know what you mean."

"In the high school yearbook you were quoted as saying you wanted to join the circus."

He retrieved the pencil, put it back in the cup, and sighed. "Oh, yes, of course. No, I didn't join the circus. I sometimes wish I had. Maybe I still could, but it will never happen. Just a kid's dream."

He eased back in his chair. His down-to-business demeanor returned. I asked him to tell me anything he knew about the

14

murder of Linsley Sinclair.

"I know nothing more than was in the newspaper," he said. "Naturally I want to know more because she was such a ... friend. I called and talked to a captain, but he said he couldn't tell me anything that wasn't in the news."

"Tell me about the grand quartet," I said.

His eyes darted around the room and settled on the office door for a few seconds. Was he expecting someone? I waited.

"Charlie Connor and I had been friends since grade school. He was so athletic, and I couldn't do much of anything. I always had spending money and candy even in grade school. Charlie loved candy.

"In high school he became a big football star right away and started dating Lins. He included me when they went places because I still supplied him with money. So he lined me up with Laura Beckert. She wasn't thrilled about it. But she liked Charlie and was willing to date me because of that, I think.

"Lins was a snob, but Charlie had fallen for her. Anyway, Lins didn't like it when others joined us for anything, even just eating lunch in the school cafeteria, so the other kids called us the 'grand quartet.'"

"What about you and Laura? Did you two become serious?"

He laughed without humor and said, "No way. She wasn't about to be my girl. Not when she could have any other guy in school except Charlie."

"Do you ever see her now?"

He fidgeted on his throne, wiped his forehead with a paper napkin, and said, "She comes into the store now and then. She is full of nice memories about us she's created since high school. I'm a successful businessman. Money makes a difference."

When I asked if he knew where I could find Charlie Connor he smiled and said, "I'm surprised you don't know. He's the Charlie who supposedly manages Charlie's, that expensive restaurant at the west end of town. It was just a big barn. He turned it into a dumpy bar and grill. Now it's big business, I guess."

"He was such a star football player, how come he didn't go to college?"

"Oh, he did. Received a scholarship to the state university, but he wouldn't study. He thought he was going to get by like he did in high school. He just flunked out. He came back and bummed around for a couple of years. Then he started the bar."

"What about his connection with Linsley Sinclair? Did that continue?"

"I guess it did, for awhile. I always thought Mister Sinclair put up the money for the bar. But I don't know for sure. Charlie wanted me to lend it to him when the banks refused, but no way. We no longer were friends."

Hubbard stared beyond me, shook his head slightly, and continued.

"I don't know what happened between Lins and Charlie. I'm sure she didn't think much of the dump Charlie was running at first and the people that hung out there. I always wondered if Mister Sinclair put up the money to get Charlie started in something Lins would approve."

"Why would he do that?"

Hubbard shrugged and said he didn't know, it was just a guess.

"Lins talked about going to Chicago and living with her dad when she got out of high school. She was going to go to college somewhere up there. I guess she did for awhile."

"How well did you know Mister Sinclair?"

He stood and said he'd told me everything that could possibly be connected with Linsley's death. He hesitated, sat down again, and said, "I suppose you'll find out anyway. The police didn't ask. I know him quite well. He owns a percentage of my furniture stores. He put up the money for expansion."

I expressed surprise that Hubbard didn't borrow the money from a bank. He said he got it cheaper from Sinclair.

As I wondered why he was providing me with all this information, he said, "I know how you solved that murder when you were working for the television station and Mister Sinclair told me to cooperate so..."

"When Linsley quit going with Charlie, did she start a relationship with someone else?"

Again Hubbard hesitated. He sighed and said, "We dated for awhile after she came back from Chicago."

He went to a filing cabinet and came back with a folder marked "Lins, high school."

There were a few photos of him with Linsley and other photos of her with various people, apparently all taken when they were in high school.

"Do you have more folders with information about Linsley?"

"Just one more," he said, "but it's private. That's all I'm going to give you, I don't care what Mister Sinclair says. Besides it has nothing to do with her murder."

It was obvious he wanted to end the interview. I thanked him and left. I never did get around to eating one of those doughnuts.

When I got back to Otto's, he said, "I have some information that may be important."

"Ya, what's dat?"

It was a poor imitation of his voice. I apologized for being a smart ass and later thanked him with enthusiasm when he gave me his "information."

He handed me an article from the newspaper that was published the same day as the story of Linsley Sinclair's murder.

"See the year the story says this guy graduated from Centrel City High. The same year that murdered girl graduated."

Otto shrank back in mock horror when my thanks for the information included a threat to kiss him.

The story was about Rudolph Sluppleman. Now a noted psychiatrist, he was in town to give a speech to local doctors. I had seen his photo with the story when I read the paper but didn't connect it later to the photo in the yearbook.

Doctor Sluppleman practiced in Chicago. Later, when I contacted him by phone, he said he would be in Centrel City again in a few days and would be available to answer any questions he could.

At the police station, Andy Brown talked on the phone for fifteen minutes while I waited. The top of his metal desk was buried in papers, folders, a couple of dirty coffee cups, a framed photo of his wife, and two teenage sons and a miniature golf bag filled with pencils and pens.

When it finally was my turn to talk, I passed on the information about Sinclair's connection to Hubbard and the fact that another high school classmate, Sluppleman, had been in town the night Linsley Sinclair was murdered.

"Well," Andy said as he gently rubbed his hairless noggin, "I owe you one. How about this? The etiquette book in the victim's lap was open to two pages about the proper way to get laid. The book was held open to those particular pages by rubber bands so it was no accident. And tracks in the cinders indicate whoever put the body in the bleachers dragged it there, probably from a car."

I started to thank him and make a smart remark about needing to know more about the etiquette of getting laid when he said, "There's more. The victim was killed by a massive dose of GHB, according to the autopsy report."

"What's GHB?"

Andy, now leaning back in his swivel chair with his feet on the edge of the desk, reached for a report and read with stumbling pronunciation, "GHB stands for gamma hydroxybutyric, of course.

The stuff is one of the so-called date rape drugs. It knocks the victim out. Now, according to a report in *Newsweek* magazine, it's used as a party drug. The stuff is dangerous. Too much is deadly. It used to be available from health food stores but not now. Still, like any drug, people find ways to get it."

I copied the spelling and went over the pronunciation aloud, practicing for my report to Sinclair.

After thanking Andy for the information and repeating my promise to keep it to myself, except for the report to Sinclair, I returned to my office.

I was annoyed by how anxious I was to impress Sinclair. I thought about the guy as I worked on my report. Sometimes, I have noted, the more obnoxious a person is the more people cater to them.

All the information I had gathered so far I would pass on to Sinclair over the phone, but I also would send him a written report. I was working on that when Maggie Atley knocked. She came into the office and accused me of not feeding the cat.

"Damn you Nick, you did it again. Mister Ballard got all over me. The cat was in the office complaining because you forgot to feed it."

"What do you mean, 'Ballard got all over you?'"

"You know what I mean. It was about the cat being in the office."

She stood in front of me, her eyes intent. Like the cat in some ways, I thought.

"I fed her. Am I going to have to come up here every morning just to check in the hallway to see if you fed her?"

"That would be nice," I agreed. "You could check on me also to see if I'm out of bed and so on."

"Please Nick, I'm serious. Mister Ballard has threatened to call animal control and get rid of the cat if I can't keep it out of the office. You did agree to feed it. I even provide the food."

She was cooing as she did when the subject first came up, and I agreed to feed the cat. That was before it occurred to me that eventually there might be any number of stray cats outside my door waiting to be fed.

However, apparently this cat, white with a patch of black on its neck and another on its tail, was smart enough not to let any of its buddies in on the free food.

Maggie sat on the chair opposite my desk with her hands in her lap and her back straight.

"I guess you have done pretty well. The cat, as you call it, is gaining weight. When I first saw it the poor thing was mostly bones."

"I've never understood your interest in this cat. You don't go around feeding all stray animals, do you?"

She said the cat looked so forlorn and hungry when it sneaked into her office she just had to feed it. And, of course, it kept coming back. She said it was just about tame enough so she could pet it when Ballard demanded that she get rid of it.

"Pets are not allowed in the apartment building where I live. I used to have a cat at home. I like cats."

I was about to say she could pet me when she said, "So this is your office. I've often wondered about it. Don't you ever sweep the floor or dust things?"

"I'm too busy for that kind of work, and my cleaning service is on strike."

"I shudder to think what that other room looks like."

"We can't have you shuddering," I said. I walked across the room and opened the door to the living quarters.

"If I'd a known you was coming I'd a made the bed," I said as I watched her hesitate before deciding to have a look.

There is the bed, a refrigerator, a television, an overstuffed chair, and a wash stand. There also is a shower enclosed by crude plastic walls and a sliding door that sticks. The hot plate on top of the refrigerator does not work.

The one window, when the shade is up, reveals the faded red bricks of an apartment building only about six feet away. My clothes are stored in a cardboard closet and a dresser. Crowded place.

"So this is where you bring all those girls at night. I'm surprised at least one of them isn't still in the bed."

I knew why she thought that about the girls. The woman who worked for Ballard before her was a snoop who wanted to get to know me better. Like a fool, I told her fantasy stories about all the other women in my life. It only made her more determined to join them. What a relief when she was replaced by Maggie.

Maggie backed out of the room like a nervous lion trainer leaving a cage and said, "You really should hire another cleaning service."

"You tell the cat I apologize, and I really will try to remember to feed it. I must get back to work. I have a client who insists on a report at four o'clock. Since he is paying I'm going to accommodate him."

After Maggie left, it took me a few minutes to get my mind

focused on the report. Once I got started again, though, it went fast enough. At one minute to four, according to my watch, I dialed the telephone number on the card Sinclair gave me.

A woman who sounded as though she had cotton stuffed in her nose answered and demanded my name.

She put me on hold. When she returned she said, "Mister Sinclair told you to call at four o'clock. You still have four minutes to wait. Want to hold or will you call back?"

I agreed to call back. I synchronized my watch with Sinclair time and waited. I drummed my fingers on the desk and shuffled the report papers.

At exactly four o'clock, Sinclair time, I called again and was put through. I reported the information I had gathered and expected him to be impressed. If he was, he didn't reveal it.

"I'll expect another call at four tomorrow."

He hung up. I fumed for a few seconds until I remembered the money. I called to check on the time and found that Sinclair time was the correct time. As I was sitting there letting drinking-hour time slip away I wondered why such a busy man would deliver the money to me personally and why he was in town then. Was he in town the night his daughter was murdered?

At Otto's I studied the report I was going to mail to Sinclair and spilled beer on it. Not a good sign. Sending a beer-stained report to Sinclair would not do. I'd have to make another copy.

I decided to go see Charlie Connor and reminded myself to keep a record of what I spent at his place so I could claim expenses. A steak dinner would be included.

A man with a gravel voice, but the manners of a hostess, informed me that Mister Connor would not be in until at least nine o'clock, if he came at all.

"I can give him a message," the man said when I asked how I could reach Connor.

I left my name and the fact that I was investigating the death of Linsley Sinclair.

"I will be at Town and Country Bowl for the next two hours starting about twenty minutes from now," I said.

I gave him the phone number there and informed him it was a place where people bowl on bowling lanes, when he asked.

Town and Country Bowl has nothing to do with the country. It was on the lower side of the business district, near the tracks as was the police station, Otto's and the rest of my neighborhood.

The building that houses it, once a warehouse, was pre World War I brick. Everything, the carpet, the chairs, the bar, looked old and worn. Everything except the lanes. They were kept clean and in tournament condition by Dave Frank, the pro there. I talked to him for a few minutes about an upcoming tournament. He was working behind the counter. A couple of teenagers were bowling, and there were some flies at the bar. Later, I was perched in the settee at lane eighteen putting on my bowling shoes when I was called to the phone. It was Charlie Connor. He said he could meet me at my convenience and offered to buy me dinner. I agreed to meet him at his restaurant in two hours and went back to my lane.

I intended to practice on the corner pins, the seven and ten, which I have a miserable habit of missing when it really counts. I stuck with the practice for awhile, but my mind wasn't on it, and I knew I was wasting my time. Bowling, after a guy reaches a certain level of competence, is mostly mental, and my mind was wandering.

I went back to the office and watched television to kill time before going to Charlie's. The cat was sitting beside the bowl in the hallway. It backed away when I approached the door, watching me intently.

"What?" I said. The cat jumped, backed away a little farther, and stared. Maybe it was thirsty. A check of my refrigerator revealed I was out of milk so I went over to Otto's and borrowed a glass of the stuff.

I poured milk in the bowl, put it in front of the open office door and sat at my desk, waiting to see if the cat would drink it.

This was a careful cat. It crept up to the bowl, spotted me inside the office, and moved away again. A few minutes later it was back, and this time it lapped the milk when it wasn't watching me. It cleaned its whiskers, took a final look at me, and came into the office.

I figured if I moved it would evaporate so I sat there like a dummy watching as the cat explored, always I think, with an eye on the door.

"Don't get the idea that you can come in here just any time," I said quietly. The cat paused, one paw in midair. It looked at me for a moment and continued moving, now back toward the door. It left the room, a silent white shadow.

As I left I thought about how it would be to have the cat as a pet. I had a dog when I was a boy. It chased cats. I never before thought of owning a cat. A dog again, maybe. Did I want the responsibility? How much trouble would a cat be?

On my way to Charlie's restaurant I thought about the questions I would ask. And about that etiquette book. I had to convince Andy to let me see it.

CHAPTER FOUR

My battered, rusting Escort looked like a poor relation among the expensive, polished cars in Charlie's Restaurant parking lot. There were plenty of parking spaces near the entrance, but I parked farther away. I didn't want one of those boats denting my little car and have the owner sue me for parking it where it didn't belong.

The barn towered over the parking lot, the cars, and me. Streaks of faded paint indicated it once had been red. The entrance included a canopy, rich red double doors, and a discrete sign that said "Charlie's" in square red letters.

I entered and was greeted by plush sofas, thick, light green carpet, and polished tables. The walls were unfinished. Lit lanterns, electrical replicas of the kind farmers once used in their barns, hung from the ceiling, giving the place a warm, friendly glow. A circular bar in the middle was surrounded by dining tables and chairs.

"Do I need a reservation," I inquired of the elegant woman who asked if I wanted smoking or nonsmoking.

She smiled, no doubt bored with such childish jokes, and said, "As you can see, this is not one of our busy nights. But if you plan to come tomorrow or during the weekend you will need a reservation."

I explained that I really was there to see Charlie.

"You are Nick Bancroft?"

When I admitted it, she said Mister Connor was waiting. She led me past the circular bar. A piano sat on a platform in the middle. No one was playing. The bartender was starting and stopping the platform by pushing an electric switch. Apparently there had been a problem. A voice from somewhere underneath said, "OK, now," and the bartender pushed the switch. The platform moved silently until it made a complete circle.

The voice from below said, "OK, that's it," as I followed the hostess around the bar.

A tall, square-jawed man with thinning hair and a ring of fat around his middle stood as we neared his table. He stuck out a big paw. I'm sure he could have squeezed my hand until I said uncle, but instead he presented a firm but friendly handshake.

"Thanks, Ruth," Connor said. The hostess moved away silently, swaying her behind.

"This is quite a place," I said as I accepted his offer to sit. "Especially when you consider it once was a barn."

"It's still a barn, just a fancied up barn," Connor said as a waitress appeared. She was undressed in a little something that resembled a bikini more than a uniform. Her legs were long and slim, her eyes were accented by lavender makeup and long, fake eyelashes. And, of course, she had prime boobs.

I ordered a glass of Michelob when I was informed they served most brands, foreign and domestic.

As I watched her move back toward the bar, I asked Charlie how they managed to keep the carpet clean what with all the traffic it must bear. He admitted he didn't have the slightest idea.

"There are people to take care of that sort of thing," he said.

I commented on the elegance of the polished tables and cushioned chairs that surrounded them, on the plush carpet, and how it all contrasted so nicely with the rugged, worn wood of the walls.

Everything I said was true, I guess, but I didn't really care. I was stalling, seeing how he would react when I didn't question him about the murder.

My beer came in a thin, tall glass that widened at the top. I sipped it like a wine taster and watched Connor who now was fidgeting with a napkin.

"You said you were investigating the death of Linsley Sinclair. Did you want to ask me some questions?"

He raised his hand, and the girl in the scant uniform appeared. The uniform was black and hugged her form like plastic wrap. He suggested I order dinner and recommended the filet mignon.

"Medium rare, house dressing, and a baked potato," I said. The waitress displayed a mouthful of white teeth and left. She didn't write any thing down, just kept it in her pretty head.

"Now, how can I help you?"

I explained that I had a copy of the high school yearbook, and as a start I was interviewing members of the grand quartet.

"Ah, yes, the grand quartet. That name was pinned on us because of Lins. She was a snob, but it was more than that. She wanted to keep things, including our group, to herself. Know what I mean?"

I asked him the usual questions about what he knew about the murder.

"Anything you can tell me might be of use."

"There is one thing no one seems to have mentioned in any of the stories I've read, and the police, when they questioned me, never mentioned it. I saw in the paper that Rudolph Sluppleman was in town the night Lins was murdered."

"So?"

"He was a member of our high school class. One day, before a big football game, Lins complained because she had to sit without a date even though Harold and Laura would be with her.

"I told Sluppleman, who was about as gullible as you can get, that Lins would appreciate it if he would sit with her in the stands during the game.

"Harold told me she became really nasty when poor old Sluppleman sat beside her. She told him the seat was taken. When he told her I said she wanted him to sit with her she told the poor slob he was the last person she ever wanted to be seen with."

"What did he do?"

"I guess he just slunk off. He seemed to tolerate being insulted. Someone was always telling him what a klutz he was. He never seemed to get it. Always hanging around trying to be one of the guys."

"Do you think he murdered Linsley?"

"Well, I don't know, of course, but I thought someone ought to know he was in town. He's a big shot doctor now. Should I tell the police, do you think?"

When I told him they knew about Sluppleman he said, "Really." He seemed surprised.

Connor left after I finished questioning him. I got the impression as he went out the front door after pausing to talk to the hostess that he came to the restaurant just to talk to me. I wondered how much he really had to do with running the place.

I ate the juicy, tender steak, the richly decorated potato, and nibbled at French peas as I sat there by myself, feeling as ostracized as Rudolph Sluppleman must have felt in high school.

A couple was seated about six tables away, two tables were occupied by lone men, and the rest of the place was empty. I noticed more activity on a carpeted, wide stairway near the front of the building that led to a second floor. Occasionally waitresses, each as scantily clad as the others, climbed the stairway. Some carried trays with drinks, and others carried nothing except their seductive frames. I never saw one return.

I would rather be at Otto's, I decided.

On the way home I stopped at a supermarket and bought a carton of milk and more cat food. I was surprised to note I was hoping the cat would be waiting for me and was disappointed when I entered my office without seeing it.

After pouring milk in the bowl and placing it on the floor near the open office door, I turned on the radio loud enough to drown out the rattle of the air-conditioner and listened to "elevator music." I was beginning to nod when the cat appeared, as silent as the dead.

It watched me for a moment and then lapped up the milk, still facing in my direction. It stopped drinking every few seconds and watched me. I pretended to be busy with papers on my desk. I'd show that cat I didn't care if it drank the milk or not.

When the milk was gone the cat backed up a few steps and cleaned its whiskers while it watched me. I slowly placed my feet on the desk and watched it.

"I've got a busy day tomorrow cat. I guess I should stop watching you and get to bed. What do you think?"

I spoke quietly, not wanting to startle this very cautious animal. As I wondered how it survived before Maggie started feeding it, the cat entered the office and began exploring. It was making a noise, purring I guess. It was about half way into the room to my left when I tried to move my feet back to the floor quietly. The cat zipped out the door before my feet touched the floor.

I sat there for a moment wondering why I was wasting my time with the cat anyway. I had a case, a murder case, and I wasn't getting anywhere. I turned off the radio. I had to concentrate.

There might be some connection between high school and the murder, I decided, but there could be a thousand other reasons why Linsley Sinclair was killed.

What about the book of etiquette? Maybe that was the only real clue. There must be some meaning there. If I couldn't get Andy Brown to let me see the book, he surely would tell me the title of the damned thing so I could buy a copy. Another item to add to the expense account.

I'd started this business of interviewing members of the grand quartet so, I decided, I might as well complete the task and interview the last one, Laura Beckert.

The air-conditioner rattled on, and, in spite of my concern that I was going to have little to tell Sinclair in my next report, I started nodding. I turned the radio back on, closed and locked the front door, and went to bed. I couldn't sleep. I thought of going over to Otto's. It was midnight, and he stayed open until one. I decided

26

against that. I had been there for the closing of too many bars. There is nothing more depressing than being with the last person to leave a bar before it closes. Especially if that person is your mother.

What about Maggie? I figured she was a woman who wouldn't fool around without some sort of commitment, and I wanted nothing to do with that.

Marriage, a family, all that stuff, didn't sound so bad except it would eliminate so many other things. All of them had to do with selfishness, as one girl said when I resisted her efforts to hog tie me.

Bowling was just one thing, but it was big with me. I loved competition, and bowling was where I competed best. Not that I was a champion. The best I ever finished in a regional professional tournament was tenth. But I loved the anticipation of trying again and of being accepted by the guys who really were good. And practicing. I loved it. I would feel guilty even if a woman would put up with my being gone half the weekends to bowl in tournaments and being gone all the time I was practicing. Now, with no commitments, I could bowl as often as I wanted, practice as often as I wanted, and spend as much time at Otto's as I wanted. And what about the dismal business I inherited? What woman would want to try to live off the money I was making?

No, I decided, Maggie you can entice me with your eyes, your slow, knowing smile, the way your hips move when you walk, all that good stuff, but I won't do it.

I finally went to sleep only to wake up to another murder.

CHAPTER FIVE

Getting up in the morning is not one of my favorite things. There's no fresh coffee. I should have bought one of those deals that turn on automatically just before you get up, and there it would be, fresh, hot coffee.

After getting the coffee started in my battered, non-automatic pot, I stepped into shorts and turned on the radio. I listened to a "golden oldies" station because it announced the major league baseball scores every fifteen minutes or so.

Being a Chicago Cub fan was a form of self torture, so my day seldom got off to a good start. Hearing again that the Cubs lost was not as painful as it once was. A person can get used to anything.

So there I was, trying to keep from burning my lips on the hot coffee and wondering if Laura Beckert would tell me anything helpful about the murder of Linsley Sinclair, when an announcer broke into a soulful rendition of a sad song and announced that Harold Hubbard was dead, apparently the victim of a murder.

His body was found, the announcer said, by an employee who opened his downtown furniture store for business. It was only about ten minutes past ten so the store could not have been open long.

The police would still be there. I dressed hurriedly, gulped some coffee, and headed for the scene.

A cop I knew guarded the store entrance. When I explained that I was investigating the Linsley Sinclair murder, that this crime, if it was one, might be connected, and that Andy Brown would want to see me, the cop – I couldn't for the life of me remember his name – let me duck under the crime-scene ribbon and enter the building.

"If Brown chews me out for letting you in it's your ass," he said.

Brown and a guy from the coroner's office were in Hubbard's office. The body was slumped in the big chair behind Hubbard's desk. It was dressed in a short-sleeved shirt and blue jeans. I couldn't see the face, but I could see an open book in the lap. It was a copy of the book found with Linsley Sinclair's body.

When I started to ask Brown about the book he told me what it was before I finished the question. We talked about my interview with the guy only the day before, and how I'd also interviewed Connor. A police photographer was shooting away and occasionally asked us to move so he could get another angle on the body.

"He's got a needle mark on one arm, like the Sinclair woman. Maybe he was killed with the same stuff," Brown said. Someone called him. I left the office and sat in one of the cushioned display chairs nearby. I was in the way in the office and tired of standing anyway.

About half an hour later Brown spotted me as he was leaving the scene. Most of the other people had gone.

"I'll want a full report on your interview with this guy and Connor on my desk by this afternoon," Brown said.

I nodded and followed him out of the building. I had stopped worrying about having something new to tell Sinclair in my next report.

Back at Otto's, I read the sports pages while Otto asked me questions about the second murder. I finally told him I was sworn to secrecy and would he please shut up so I could read.

"Ya, you've got the big case of your life, and all you want to do is read the sports pages."

"When I have time," I said, "I'll give you all the details I have gathered and you can analyze them and solve the case. In the meantime, let me chew on this month-old doughnut and catch up on the sports news. I see the Cubs lost again."

"Ya, like that's news."

I spent the rest of the morning writing reports of my interviews with Hubbard and Connor. I described the reactions to my questions and recalled every detail I could about what they said. I wanted to give Brown as much information as possible. Maybe it would help him solve the case and remove the pressure from me.

After making copies of the reports to mail to Sinclair, I called ex-mayor Beckert's retirement residence in Florida, seeking a way to contact Laura Beckert. A young man, maybe a teenager, answered the phone and said Laura, "his aunt," did not live there. He hung up before I could ask if he knew where she lived.

I had a brilliant idea. I looked in the local telephone book, and, behold, there was her name, telephone number, and address. There was no answer to the many calls I made to the number that afternoon. I gave up and went to the police station with my reports. I had to get the Brown meeting out of the way so I could call Sinclair at exactly four o'clock. The guy had me dancing to his tune.

Brown thanked me for the reports, said he appreciated my cooperation, and added, "We thought Linsley Sinclair might have been raped, but she wasn't. That book is entitled 'Sex Etiquette, how to do it right.'"

"Thanks. Got any suspects?"

He didn't answer my question but did say, after I explained my problem with getting in touch with Laura Beckert, that police were having the same trouble.

"She could be in danger, you know, and Connor too," Brown said. "She was a member of this group mentioned in the yearbook. If you find her let us know, right?"

I agreed and hurried back to my office. Didn't want to be late with the call. Maggie knocked on my door. She entered when I waved her in from my stretched out position behind the desk. She put her hands on her hips and said, "You forgot to feed Ruffles this morning. Really Nick, you promised."

I lowered my feet, bowed, and apologized.

"To think I let a little thing like a murder cause me to forget to feed the cat. I'm devastated. Ruffles, you've named that scraggly cat 'Ruffles?'"

"She's not scraggly."

"She?"

"Well, maybe, I don't know."

"I've got to make an important phone call. Would you mind taking your tantalizing presence out of here so I can stop thinking about cat feeding and, and ... er ... other things."

Her eyes widened for an instant. She appeared to be thinking of replying but, instead, turned and left, closing the door with a bang.

My timing must have been correct because I was put through to Sinclair immediately. After describing everything I had done since our last talk I reported details of the second murder.

"Harold Hubbard is dead?"

I agreed that he was and waited for further comment from him.

He said, "Do you think his death is connected to Linsley's murder?"

When I said I didn't know, he told me to find out.

"Don't waste your time with Connor. He isn't involved, I'm sure. Don't you or the police have any suspects yet?"

"Not really. There are some possibilities but..."

"I don't want possibilities; I want to know who killed my daughter. Stay on it. There's a bonus if you find out who did it."

He hung up before I could reply. A bonus would be nice. But

how could he know Charlie Connor had nothing to do with his daughter's death?

CHAPTER SIX

"Ya, what are you going to do now, hotshot? Just sit around and read the sports pages? You don't have a clue as to how to solve these murders," Otto said.

I was trying to concentrate on how the Cubs had managed to win a game. If I admitted I had no real clues as to who committed the murders, he would start giving me advice. The guy who left me the business, Jimmie Jackson, used to spend some time in Otto's joint, and Otto was full of stories about how Jimmie solved various cases, with his help.

Jimmie told me some of the same stories, but there was quite a difference between the two versions.

I had looked at Jimmie's files. Most were just routine records of boring cases, but some, the ones Otto loved to talk about, were interesting even if they were not as exciting as Otto remembered.

One file was labeled "Charlie's." The only thing in it was a sheet of paper with a large, penciled question mark on it. What question did Jimmie have about the place?

Otto's doughnuts were fresher than usual. I was thinking of having another, but he was getting on my nerves.

"I've got to go. Got to run down some new leads," I told him.

"Ya, some new leads, ha."

I went across the street to my office. I had forgotten again to feed the cat. I put some food in its bowl and watched from my desk. The cat appeared in only a few seconds and ate the food, paying little attention to me.

After his majesty left, I thought about Maggie as I tried to concentrate on the reason why a murderer would place a sex etiquette book in the laps of the victims, one male, one female.

I was leaving when the three young toughs who had accosted BJ blocked my way out. I hadn't heard them climbing the stairs, but there they were.

"To what do I owe this pleasure?" I said as they pushed into my office.

The biggest one, his finger poking at me as he talked, said, "That goofy old fart you protected the other day, he's trying to

32

clean up that alley. He says we should help. We ain't doin' nothin' unless you do. Put up or shut up. You said we should clean up the alley. How about it?"

They wouldn't buy my insistence that I had my own work to do. The littlest guy – his hair colored red and green and cropped short – bared yellow teeth and said, "I told you this honky wouldn't help us. Let's get out of here. We got stuff to do besides clean up an old alley."

"Are you jerks trying to lure me back to that alley so you can pound the shit out of me, is that it?"

"Why don't you come along and see? You scared? You can watch the old guy work if you is too lazy to do it. He thinks he's on a holy mission, like a crusader," the big guy said.

I worried about what they might have done to BJ so I followed them out of the building to the alley, ready to defend myself if they jumped me. What I had to do, I decided, was get a permit to carry a gun. Maybe it was too late.

I could hear BJ singing before we reached him. He had carried wine bottles, cans, and other debris to a large cardboard box near the entrance. He clutched a pair of half-rotted men's shoes as he looked at me and smiled.

"This is fun, Mister Nick. Are you going to help?"

Three new rakes and an old shovel were propped against a faded red brick wall. I didn't ask where they got the rakes.

"I'll be damned," I said.

"Are you going to help or not?" big man demanded.

All three of the young faces turned toward me.

I picked up a rake. BJ and big man joined me as we raked leaves, newspapers, bones of a small animal, and years of debris that had rotted into a smelly muck. The little guy replaced Mister Big. We dragged the increasingly heavy mess about half way to the alley opening. The little guy said it was time for a break. He wiped sweat from his pimpled face with a dirty shirt sleeve.

We leaned on the rakes. The biggest guy took the rake from BJ, and the third guy relieved his buddy. We dragged the increasing pile toward the front. I was breathing hard, and we still had several yards to go.

I stopped, leaned on the rake handle, and said, "What do we do with this mess when we get to the end of the alley?"

The guy who hadn't said a word spoke up. He was almost as tall as the biggest one but not as thick. He had long, greasy black hair, a mustache, and a two-day-old beard. He stuttered but managed to say that he wasn't going to stay around and haul this shit anywhere. "Just leave it here," he insisted.

I started raking again, and the others joined in. When we got the pile near the opening the biggest guy said,

"Mister hot shot here, Mister clean, you got connections ain't you? You just call city hall, and they send a truck right away. Isn't that right?"

Black holes from his missing teeth showed as he grinned. We all stood for a moment looking into the clean alley.

"It looks keen don't it, Mister," BJ said. It did. I felt a glimmer of pride.

"I'll call city hall. I think I know a guy who will break his ass getting a truck here because of the publicity."

It seemed to satisfy them. I told BJ it was time to leave. I still didn't trust these guys and still didn't know their names.

After walking BJ home, I stopped at Waldenbooks store and called Street Commissioner Al Gordon. He agreed to send someone to haul the junk away. He asked questions and seemed disappointed when I couldn't tell him the names of the three who had helped.

At Waldenbooks, I cornered a clerk who found a copy of *Sex Etiquette.* I bought it, made a note for the expense account, and kept the receipt.

I noted the pile of trash with a feeling of satisfaction as I walked back into my neighborhood and to my car. Soon I was in a different world, a world without visible junk, as I drove on West Palmer Avenue by Lake Goshen to Laura Beckert's apartment building. The neighborhood featured weedless, manicured lawns.

After parking across the street from the apartment building, I opened the book to the pages Andy Brown had told me were the ones exposed at both murders.

It was a chapter telling the reader that force was not acceptable behavior in sexual relations. I was anxious to read on but had to check first on which apartment was Laura's.

In the carpeted hall of the building I learned Laura's apartment was number 205. I buzzed just in case, but when there was no answer after a few minutes, I gave up and returned to my car. I had no idea which window was connected to Apartment 205 so I just watched the entrance to the building.

Would I recognize Laura Beckert if I saw her? I had the yearbook open to her photo. In it she had a round, plump face with quiet eyes and light brown hair. Her lips were full and sensuous.

Stakeouts are a pain in the ass, sometimes literally, and more often than not, nonproductive. I was trying to watch the entrance

34

to the building and read the etiquette book at the same time.

The gist of the part of the book involved was that a person, under no circumstances, should use force or take advantage of a person who was incapacitated because of drugs or booze.

What connection could that have with Linsley Sinclair? A man like Harold Hubbard might do such a thing but a woman? I had to find out more about Linsley's past. And Hubbard's. Did they have a past together? Maybe the answer was to be found there. I felt a sense of urgency brought on by Ramsey Sinclair's intimidating manner.

After an hour and a half of watching the entrance I saw no one resembling the photo of Laura Beckert. I was about to leave and get another cup of keep-me-awake coffee when I saw a face I recognized.

It was Rudolph Sluppleman. He parked a black Lincoln in front of the building, got out, and went in. I was leaning against his car when he came out only a minute or so later.

"Still trying to find out why people are so inhumane?" I asked as he neared his car.

He wasn't much more than five feet tall, but his tailored clothes, his close-cropped black hair, a neatly trimmed black mustache, and eyes that bore through thick black-rimmed eyeglasses into a person's soul made him seem taller.

"Who are you?"

He reminded me of a bantam rooster challenging a cock twice its size.

"My name is Nick Bancroft. I'm investigating the murders of two high school classmates of yours and have been trying to contact Laura Beckert. Apparently you're trying to do the same."

"What was that question you asked me? Oh, you must have seen the high school yearbook. Yes, I'm still trying to learn more about the reasons why people do the awful things they do to themselves and each other."

"Do you have time for a cup of coffee? I called you, remember, about an interview."

He pushed his silk suit sleeve up to reveal a glittering wristwatch, looked at it, and said he did have time.

"I was going to call and tell you I was in town. There is a coffee shop on the other side of this block. Could we walk? I need the exercise."

I had to hustle to keep up with this little man. His arms swung, and his heals clicked rapidly.

"Now, how may I help you?" he said as he slid into a booth in the "Happy Hour Diner."

The diner was squeezed between two brick and glass buildings. It glistened with steel counters and a black and white tile floor.

I took a deep breath and said, "Have you been in contact with members of the group called the grand quartet or any one else who might have something to do with all of this?"

"I've seen Charlie Connor a few times since I left to go to college. He is connected with that expensive restaurant on the edge of town."

"What do you mean, connected?"

"I doubt that he owns it. Someone is using his name because he was such a football star and still, I suppose, appeals to women. But he is not the kind of person who could raise that much money, and I can't imagine him actually managing the business."

"What about the others?"

"I was at a party once in Chicago. When I discovered Linsley Sinclair was there, I left. I had an unpleasant experience with her in high school and didn't have any desire to see her again."

His eyelids lowered and his smile vanished when I told him what I knew about Charlie setting him up for Linsley's scorn during a football game.

"I've come a long way since then. I was such a trusting fool. It still amazes me how I could be uncomfortable now about meeting that venomous bitch, Linsley Sinclair. I'm as bad as many of my patients. I guess I'll never be able to erase some teenage experiences."

"What about Laura Beckert? Have you kept in touch with her?"

He was quiet for a few seconds and then spoke as though he was on trial.

"I have seen her, yes, on and off over the years."

"Where do you suppose she is now? I haven't been able to reach her."

He put his hand on his chin and stared at the floor.

"She could be visiting her son. She claims she has a son. Frankly, I doubt it."

"She might be in danger, if these murders have anything to do with high school. Is she your patient?" I said.

He was silent.

"You were in town the night Linsley Sinclair was killed and apparently also when Harold Hubbard was killed. Do police know you're in town now?"

"That is one reason why I'm here. I'm going to go to the police station and talk to Sergeant Andrew Brown. I've already contacted him."

Sluppleman said he would appreciate it if I kept him informed after he went back to Chicago. He gave me a business card which included his unlisted home telephone number.

After he left, I watched the entrance to the apartment building until noon and gave up. I went to the court house and checked on the ownership of a piece of land for another client.

Back at the office, I called the client, Jason Williams. He thanked me and promised to send a check. That's the kind of conversation I like.

"If you had a felt hat pulled over your eyes and a bottle of booze on your desk you would look like a real detective, at least a movie detective," Maggie Atley said a few minutes later as she stood in the doorway to my office. "May I come in?"

My feet were on the desk, and I was nearly asleep. I sat up, rubbed my eyes, and motioned for her to enter. She was carrying a paper bag.

"I brought us sandwiches and coffee for lunch, if your schedule will allow it," she said as her gaze covered the room.

"Are you looking for something?"

"I thought maybe Ruffles might be here," she said.

"Then you didn't come to see me. Thanks for the sandwich and coffee anyway."

It was a hamburger crammed with all the trimmings, just the way I liked it. And the coffee, it was rich and flavorful, a tremendous improvement over the stuff I occasionally brewed and better by far than the stuff Otto called coffee.

She pulled the "guest" chair up to my desk. We sat across from each other eating and smiling.

"This is a pleasant surprise, and if I could I would produce the cat. It only shows up when I offer food. I fed it this morning. I remembered. Is that worth a kiss or something?"

She carefully placed her half-eaten sandwich on the desk, wiped her hands on a napkin and stood. She took a deep breath, came around to my side of the desk, took my face in her hands, and kissed me. Her lips were warm and nerve tingling as she pressed our mouths together and held them there.

Before I could grab her she swiveled away gracefully, glided around the desk, sat down, and took a bite out of what remained of her sandwich.

"Now tell me about your exciting work."

I answered her many questions until she seemed satisfied.

"This is the best lunch I've had in a long time," I said.

Her eyes sparkled as she wiped crumbs from her face and sipped coffee.

"To what do I owe the pleasure?"

Her mouth was full, and I waited as she chewed on my question as well as the sandwich.

"I'm not sure. It was spontaneous, maybe just to pay you back for the surprise you gave me the other day when you kissed me."

I was wondering what kind of commitment this might be leading me into when she laughed, a pleasant sound, like the music of gently nudged wind chimes.

"Stop worrying. I'm not going to trap you into losing your freedom. I've got some freedom of my own to protect. Why must men always take everything so seriously? Why can't we just enjoy each other and let it go at that?"

"Yeah, sure, have your way with my body and then go on your merry way, leaving me with the consequences," I said.

More musical laughter filled the room. She stood, gathered up the empty coffee cups, napkins, and sandwich wrappers, put them in the paper bag, and said, "I'll come up here again sometime ... to see Ruffles. Maybe some evening after I get off work."

She was gone before I managed to mumble, "Do that."

I paced the floor for awhile, trying to understand her actions. Maybe I should find out more about her. Yeah, forget the murder you're paid to investigate and the other one that apparently is connected. Forget that and investigate Maggie Atley because she kissed you. I paced and didn't notice the cat until I sat down again. It was sitting at attention just outside the open office door.

Ruffles? It didn't fit this little beast that appeared now and then like a stray thought. When I stood, determined to do something besides think about Maggie, the cat streaked away into the shadows.

I decided to be more like the cat. Get off my ass and do something. As I saw it, I had three choices. I could go over to Otto's and try to talk him into selling me a beer before the designated hour, go stake out Laura Beckert's apartment building again, or practice bowling.

I decided on the bowling. It wasn't the complete waste of time it might seem. Since I was a kid I have spent a lot of time practicing bowling and thinking at the same time. Perhaps that is the reason why I'm not better at bowling than I am. At times my mind wanders.

Going to bowling lanes used to be my relief from facing problems at home. Now it was a way to avoid problems or, when I was lucky, solve them.

As I took joy in the sound of the ball smashing into the pins and knocking them all down, I tried to examine what it was that had been bugging me since ... when?

I was in the third game, where I just shoot at the corner pins, when I missed the seven pin again. It pissed me off. I'm left-handed. That's the reason why the seven pin is the most difficult to cover for me whereas for the right-hander it's the ten pin.

I sat down in disgust, knowing it was just a matter of concentration and execution to knock the damned pin down.

My mind abandoned the thought and up popped the thing that had been bugging me. What goes on upstairs at Charlie's restaurant?

Whores? Gambling? Maybe both. What difference did it make to me? It had nothing to do with Linsley Sinclair's murder, did it?

I decided to learn more about Laura Beckert. Harold Hubbard would have been an easy place to start if he were alive. And her father, the ex-mayor, could be helpful except he had retired to Florida.

It would have to be Charlie, at least for starters. He might know Laura's history since high school and maybe even how I could reach her. I should have asked him more about her when we talked before. And he didn't give me much information when I asked him about his relationship with Linsley Sinclair.

When I called the restaurant I was informed that Charlie probably was playing golf, but they would get the message to him, and he would call me.

Back at the office I prepared notes for my call to Sinclair and wrote a report on my latest activities.

When I made the call he seemed uninterested, and I expected an explosion from his end because of my lack of progress in finding out who killed his daughter. Instead he said again there was no reason for me to be wasting my time – and his – investigating that damned restaurant.

"If I wanted you to investigate a restaurant I would have said so. I want to know who killed my daughter."

I was thinking of asking if he minded if I looked into the activities at the restaurant on my own time just to see what he would say. He hung up before I could.

It was past four o'clock, and I should have been over at Otto's drinking a cold beer. Instead I was sitting in my office actually thinking of dusting the radio and window sill.

There was plenty of paper work to do involving the few other cases I still was working on, and my bookkeeping was behind. I was about to do something when the cat appeared at the open office door.

"No milk for you now, cat," I announced.

It listened, apparently without much interest, and when I put my feet down from the desk it didn't run. The phone rang. As I reached for it, I watched the cat's tail go out of sight beyond the door.

The background noise made it difficult for me to understand the caller. It was Charlie. After hearing him shout some obscenities the noise level diminished to the point where I learned he was in the clubhouse of a golf course.

"I'm drinking up, er breaking up, a big card game to call you Bancroft, what do you want now?"

I explained I had more questions, but perhaps now wasn't the time to talk to him.

"Now is a great time, I'm going to hang around here for a few more drinks, and, if you get on your horse right away, you'll be here before I leave."

"Where are you?"

"At the golf course, I told you."

"What golf course?"

He thought it was hilarious that I didn't know which golf course and finally said it was the golf course across from his restaurant.

"Does it have a name?"

"Sure, Hillcrest, just across the road, well it's about a mile south on the road just across from the restaurant. You can't miss it."

I didn't miss it, but I was lucky. There was a small sign, partially obscured by a tree branch, that whispered "Hillcrest."

After driving up a winding, freshly resurfaced blacktop, I came upon a spacious, recently remarked parking lot. It was next to a one-story, sprawling brick building with a huge window that looked out on a putting green.

Beyond the green was the first tee. I knew because I could see the sign saying "No. 1," and another sign diagramming the layout of the hole.

The parking lot, clubhouse, putting green and No. 1 tee were at the crest of a hill overlooking a valley. Golf carts, golfers, greens, and tree-lined fairways were visible below. Again my Escort looked out of place among the bigger cars in the lot. At the far end, away from the clubhouse, were some older, smaller cars. Probably belonged to employees. I parked there.

In the clubhouse I was directed by a waitress past the picture window, several tables and chairs, some occupied by men and women in casual wear, to the bar where the man in charge informed me Charlie was in the card room. He pointed to a door which, indeed, said "Card Room."

Charlie sat by himself near a corner at a round, felt-covered table. Cards were scattered over it, and Charlie fumbled with part of a deck, mumbling to himself. He seemed happy to see me.

"They all left. I wasn't even winning. They just got up and left. I insist on buying you a drink."

"There is no need to insist. I would love a cold beer."

He pushed a button on the side of the table, and a waitress appeared. She took my order and Charlie's. She picked up three shot glasses from near Charlie and moved away silently on the carpeted floor.

"You know I really cared about Lins. She was my first love. In high school. She was a bitch, even I knew that, but when we were alone sometimes she could be nice, you know what I mean?"

I nodded, not wanting to say the wrong thing and stop him from talking, not so much to me, but to himself.

"She warned me not to get involved with her dad, said he would just use me. She was right. But why did she have to leave me? She was too ambitious, that was it. She didn't want to be married to anyone who would be a front for her dad's deals."

He was slumped in his chair. He sat up and complained because the damned chairs wouldn't slide on the carpet like chairs should at a card table. His eyes were red and moist.

"You said you wanted something. More questions, that was it, wasn't it?"

I nodded, and, when he told me to ask away I tried to guide him into telling me more about his relationship with Linsley.

"No," he said, "that's personal and a long time ago. I ain't tellin' you. It's none of your business, none of the police's business either."

I was about to remind him there was a murder involved but decided it might upset him and cause him to clam up. So I said, "Maybe you could tell me more about what's happened to Laura Beckert since high school. The police are looking for her and so am I. She might even be in some danger. After all both murder victims were part of that high school group. And what about you? Maybe you're in danger. Did you guys do anything to anybody that would make them want to kill? Besides what you did to Sluppleman, I mean."

He sat up straighter as he said, "We didn't do nothing to

nobody, who told you we did?" He looked around the room as if the walls were closing in on him.

If I didn't say the right thing, I was about to lose him. I probably would never get another opportunity like this to get him talking freely. I mentioned football. We talked, or rather he did, about his high school exploits, and how he could have been an all-America player in college if they would have let him play.

"I suppose keeping up the grades was hard. I'm surprised they didn't have someone help you study."

"Laura tried to help, but that stuff isn't for me. All I wanted to do was play football, not read some pissy ass book."

"Laura? Laura Beckert?"

"Yeah, she followed me to college. She's been following me ever since high school."

When I asked him again if he knew how I could get in touch with her, he told me to go to the restaurant and talk to the head hostess. "She can tell you where Laura is."

Apparently there was a joke in there somewhere because he laughed and refused to share the reason why.

When he said he wasn't going to answer any more questions, but tried to order me another drink, I told him I had to leave.

"Go ahead and leave. Like all the others, I don't care."

At the restaurant I asked the woman who greeted me for the head hostess and explained what Charlie had told me. She picked up a phone from the reservation desk and talked to someone. She was like all the others. Long legs, made up face, skimpy costume and prime boobs.

"Miss Romano will be out in a moment," she informed me. Pointing to one of the plush benches provided for those in waiting, she invited me to sit.

Miss Romano turned out to be the elegant woman who was there the night I first talked to Charlie. I had a chance to examine her more closely as she approached. She carried herself like a professional model, swaying gently and gliding as she walked. She smiled in my direction, as though I was a long lost friend. But there was no smile in her eyes. They were the kind you see in people who have observed too much.

When she passed under the light at the reservation desk her dark hair glistened. I noted lighter hair at the roots. "How may I help you?"

"I'm looking for Laura Beckert. Charlie said I should ask you. He said you would know where she is. He seemed to think it was a joke."

"He would, the bastard. I suppose he's drunk over at the golf course."

I nodded and asked her if he would be able to get home all right or if I should go back and try to talk him into letting me drive him.

"What do you want with Laura Beckert?"

She sat on the bench beside me. The aroma was subtle, enticing. Her hands were manicured to the last cuticle. No rings on her fingers.

She wasn't in the bare-the-flesh costume she wore the first night I saw her. Still, her dress revealed enough to interest any breathing male.

"I'm trying to find Laura Beckert to question her about the murder of Linsley Sinclair and maybe Harold Hubbard."

"What else did Charlie tell you?"

"Not much. Do you know where Laura Beckert is?" She brushed a hand over her hair, wet her lips and sighed.

"Who are you?"

I explained my connection with Linsley's father.

"That bastard hired you? I'm surprised he cares."

"Do you know him?"

"I'm Laura Beckert. But now I call myself Ruth Romano.

My dad, you know the great ex-mayor, said it would sully his precious name if people knew his daughter was working at a place like this. So I changed my name.

"Poor Harold, Lins treated him like a dog. I don't understand what men see in a woman like that. She thought her shit didn't stink, like she was better than everybody else, pardon the expression."

I asked her about the incident at the football game when Charlie Connor set up Rupert Sluppleman.

"That's the way she was," Laura-Ruth said. "Poor Red Nose was devastated, but he didn't get angry. He just left. I wouldn't be surprised if he was attracted to Linsley even after that."

"Do you see Doctor Sluppleman often?"

She got up from the bench, glided a few steps, and came back.

"I've got to get back to work. Ruth Romano doesn't see any of those people, except Charlie, any more. You don't need to worry about him getting home. One of those bimbos that work in the clubhouse will take care of him."

I sat there for a few minutes, watched a bikini-clad waitress float up the stairway as she balanced a tray of drinks. I got up, walked over to the stairway, and started climbing. My feet didn't make a sound on the carpeted steps. Before I got halfway up that gravely voice I remembered from my first call to the restaurant ordered me to stop.

I stopped. Looking down I saw a large man with puffy cheeks, a five-o'clock-shadow, and hostile eyes.

"I was looking for the rest rooms," I said.

"They are not up there ... sir. See the sign."

He pointed to a red neon sign below me on the main floor. It was complete with arrows and was hard to miss by anyone going up the stairs. I tried to act embarrassed because I hadn't seen it. His expression told me he didn't buy it.

After coming back down, I went by the guy, smiling up at him weakly as I passed. I imagined his eyes following me into the men's room. I half expected him to shake me while I was shaking it.

Sitting in my car after I left, I was more determined than ever to find out what went on in that place that reeked of luxury but didn't seem to have enough business to sustain it, at least not on the main floor.

Back at the office, I called Andy Brown and told him where to find Laura Beckert. He thanked me for the information and asked me to come to the station when I could because he had some stuff he wasn't going to tell me on the phone.

I asked him what he knew about the second floor at Charlie's restaurant. He was silent.

"Are you still there," I asked.

"Got to go Nick, we'll talk later."

After putting my feet on the desk in my office and stretching to get comfortable, I thought about turning on the radio but decided it was too much effort.

I realized, after a few minutes, that I was watching for the cat. And I was thinking about Maggie. Poor lonely old man. I stood up and headed for Otto's.

CHAPTER SEVEN

"You know you're getting old when..." You've heard some of the jokes tied to that statement. But the next morning was no joke to me. The night before, when the customers thinned out at Otto's, he and I argued about the case.

I drank a few more beers than is wise for an "old" man, and when I awoke I began paying for the folly of my stupid ways. The room was swaying a little, and my head was hurting a lot.

Otto had been peeved because I wouldn't tell him some of the stuff I'd promised Brown to keep to myself. Like the business about the etiquette books.

He offered several theories about the significance of the books. He also said I was on the wrong track, questioning the high school connections.

"These murders have nothing to do with high school. You know it; you're just taking the easy way. I can tell you don't have solid evidence against anyone. Ya, you're treating this case like it was a news story, interviewing everybody. Why don't you do some digging? Look up records, stuff like that."

"What records?"

"How should I know? You're the detective."

And so it went. It was late when I got home, and I had forgotten to give the cat any milk. I put it out and sat at my desk to see if it came to drink it. When I awoke the milk was gone, there was no cat around, and my neck was bent out of shape.

Maggie gave me her usual cheerful smile and greeting when I walked past her office. "I forgot to feed your damned cat," I said. Her smile faded.

At the police station, Andy Brown gave me a cup of coffee and after discussing my red eyes and lack of a shave he said, "We've got some evidence that links this Sluppleman guy to the scene of both crimes."

I placed the coffee cup carefully on his desk. Worry over my dying condition faded as I said, "Really, what evidence?"

"At the woman's death scene we found a ball-point pen with his name and fingerprints on it, and we found his fingerprints on the etiquette book at the furniture store.

Brown described the meeting he had with Sluppleman and said, "He's a cool customer. He claims he was not near the scene of either murder. He's gone back to Chicago."

"You didn't tell him about the evidence?"

Brown admitted he didn't and said he hoped he hadn't given the guy an opportunity to fly the coop.

"Why didn't you charge him?"

I'd forgotten my headache by then, but Brown had one of his own. He said he felt like a fool letting the guy go but had asked Chicago police to keep an eye on him.

"He hasn't made any run for it yet, as far as I know.

I probably will have to arrest Sluppleman and charge him soon unless something else turned up. I don't like it. He had a pen in his suit pocket similar to the one found at the scene. When I asked about it he gave it to me. Said he had a box of them in his office.

"It's too pat. Anybody could get their hands on one of those pens, apparently. I'm not so sure about the fingerprints on the book though. What do you think?"

I explained how my interviews had revealed that he had a possible motive for murdering Linsley Sinclair, but I had learned nothing that would indicate a motive for murdering Hubbard. And the etiquette books, what did they mean?"

"They could just be something to lead us from the real motive," Brown said.

My stomach, forgotten in the interest generated by the conversation, grabbed my attention again. By the time I walked to Otto's and was nursing a cup of stale coffee, I was as miserable as ever.

Otto drank at least as much as I did the night before but the old fart didn't reveal any sign of a hangover. Maybe he was hiding it. I hoped so.

"Why don't you have a doughnut? I'll give you one on the house," he said. His grin was evil.

Back at my office, I thought about a few things I could be doing, none of them helpful in the investigation of the murders. I even rejected the idea of practicing bowling. I left my living quarters door open, flopped on the bed, and hoped I could go to sleep.

It was afternoon when I awoke, turned on the radio, and realized I felt much better. It was almost time to call Sinclair. I did have the news about the evidence against Sluppleman to report so I made the call without concern.

He listened to my report on Sluppleman and *fired me*.

I was stunned. The evidence didn't mean Sluppleman was guilty. Surely, he could see it was too convenient.

When I protested, he said, "I told you to lay off snooping around that damned restaurant. And you blabbed to everyone that I hired you. That's privileged information. Just drop it. You've been paid well enough for your time. Now forget it."

He hung up.

A new experience. I'd never been fired before. Of course it was different than being fired from a full-time job, but still, I was fired.

It was a serious blow to my ego, so serious that I began dusting the window sill after moving the radio. I might even have washed the window if Maggie hadn't knocked.

I let her in after hiding the rag I was using as a dust cloth. She looked delectable, like a fresh peach. Good enough to eat.

When I offered, she sat in the chair behind my desk. I took the "guest" chair and said, "I was just going to feed the cat, want to watch?"

She put her feet on the desk, leaned back, and smiled.

"You mean you haven't fed poor Ruffles yet. She's learning what it means to depend on a male."

I put some food in the bowl and placed it just inside the office. We sat there like two kids waiting for the circus to begin.

"The cat will show up sooner or later, usually sooner but, in the meantime what can I do for you?"

She probed me about my investigation, even asking me what I was doing at Charlie's, and would I take her there sometime. She removed her feet from my desk, stood up, stretched, and said, "Do you dance?"

I did a couple of clumsy "dance" steps and said, "No, but maybe you can teach me."

She turned up the radio and held her arms out. I wondered if this was a human version of a spider web as I rubbed against her.

"You have to stop squeezing me if you want to dance," she said. Her breath, as she laughed, tickled my ear.

I can dance, or at least I thought I could, but it was fun pretending I couldn't. Her chest bounced off my chest every chance I got to make it happen, and soon we were just holding each other and swaying to the music.

Did I lead her toward the bedroom or did she lead me? Either way, that's where we wound up. She pushed me onto the bed on my back and unbuttoned my shirt. She rubbed her lips on mine, went lower, and after tickling my ears and nipples she licked my stomach.

She unzipped my pants, spread them, and said "Oh my. I'm glad you don't wear shorts."

All the while I was fumbling with her blouse without much success. She went to the end of the bed, removed my shoes and socks, and pulled my pants off. I managed to get out of the shirt. She flopped onto her back beside me and said, "Now it's your turn."

I unbuttoned her blouse, opened it like she'd opened my shirt, fumbled with her brassiere until I bared her breasts, and kissed them. Her hands tickled my balls and attachment while she unzipped her skirt. I helped her out of it, my butt near her face. She wrapped her arms around it, pulled it to her face. We tried to outdo each other in creating moist thrills. Eventually I wound up on top of her, our faces together. Our moans intermingled.

During a pause, I heard a purring sound. I placed my head against a comfortable place on her chest and nibbled, but the purring wasn't coming from her. I slid over her moist body to the edge of the bed in time to see the cat leave the room at a leisurely pace.

"The cat was here," I whispered into one of her wonderful ears.

"I know," she sighed.

I melted into an exhausted sleep with her on top of me, one of her breasts resting on my mouth. When I awoke she was gone.

CHAPTER EIGHT

At Otto's bar later that night I ignored chatter from Otto, chatter from the radio, and chatter from the customers scattered about the place. Maggie was gone. And I would have taken her out to eat, maybe to Charlie's restaurant.

We hadn't talked of love, but I thought it was understood we would see each other again. Wasn't it? As I thought about it I began to feel ... used? What kind of a game was she playing?

My mind wandered from Maggie to the fact that I had been fired. But there was another thing that kept intruding on my self-pity. I had to find out what was going on at Charlie's. It could be a big story worth money to one of the Chicago papers if I got it to them before anyone else had it.

"Did you hear that?" Otto exclaimed.

"What?"

"On the radio. They arrested Rupert Sluppleman. He's accused of both murders. You know. That case you used to have. Thought you might be interested whenever you recover from the daze you're in. It's a woman, isn't it? Maybe the one that was in here the other day?"

I thought about Andy Brown and how he said the evidence against Sluppleman was too pat. Sluppleman seemed too intelligent to drop an incriminating pen at a murder scene and leave his fingerprints at another.

"I'm sorry I interrupted your day dreaming, don't talk to me," Otto growled.

So we talked. I told him all I knew about the case. My promise to keep the information Brown fed me was off now that Sluppleman had been arrested. The whole story would be all over television and in the newspapers.

Eventually we ran out of conversation, and Otto was busy serving drinks to the customers that drifted in and out. I said good night and went back to my office.

The scent of Maggie and her perfume remained. A scratching noise at the office door got me to my feet. I opened it, expecting to see the cat. Nothing. I picked up the bowl and stood there like a fool for a few minutes. I filled the bowl with milk, and put it inside the office a few feet. The cat appeared after I returned to the desk and put my feet up. It glanced at me, sat down next to the bowl, and lapped milk. When the milk was gone the cat came nearer to me than it ever had before and was making that little rumbling noise. The purring reminded me of Maggie. The cat came around the desk and walked under my outstretched legs. It completed the circle and went leisurely out the door.

The next morning at Otto's I was trying to read the sports pages, but nothing grabbed my interest. I was planning to go to the police station and talk to Andy Brown. I wanted to find out what he knew about the upstairs at Charlie's.

Someone tapped gently on my shoulder. I turned and looked into the wrinkled face of a man just over five feet tall. His hair was gray and unruly. No hair coloring. His eyebrows were thick. He had a serious, no nonsense air about him. An elf without a sense of humor, I thought.

"Are you Nick Bancroft?" His voice was rich and powerful, as though it came from a much larger man.

"I am," I said.

"I'm Rupert Sluppleman's attorney. He's going to be arraigned later today. He wants me to hire you to find evidence to help clear him of the charges. I understand you already are investigating the murders for Ramsey Sinclair."

"He fired me yesterday," I announced.

"Good. That way there won't be any conflict of interest. Do you want the job?"

I explained my lack of a private investigator's license and how I had made little real progress in the case so far.

"Well, as I said, Mister Sluppleman wants you on the case. I'll get a retainer to you as soon as I can. In the meantime I'm going to have my own investigator come down here and see what she can dig out. I'll have her contact you."

I thought of protesting, but I had the feeling that any protest I made would be useless. He handed me a business card and left. His name was Fremont Randolph, a big name for such a little man.

"Well, you're working on something besides traffic accidents again, congratulations," Otto said.

"He's going to send his own investigator down here. She's going to contact me. I work alone, damn it."

"Not any more," Otto smirked. "Maybe she will be a knockout and can cause you all kinds of trouble with whatever woman has you ga ga at the moment. Ya, look on the bright side."

While walking to the police station, I wondered what I could do for Sluppleman to earn my money. I had the feeling that he was innocent but...

Andy Brown offered me coffee which I took as a friendly gesture, even though I had no intention of drinking the stuff. After telling him I had a new client I admitted I had no new leads on the murders. I asked what he knew about the upstairs at Charlie's restaurant.

"I'm not convinced that Sluppleman is guilty, but the powers that be wanted charges filed. Good luck in finding more evidence. Our investigation is continuing, unofficial like."

Silence. All the police station activity of night arrests and hassles was over, and it was too early for another round to start.

I shifted in my chair, stood up, stretched, and said, "Well, I guess you're not going to answer my question about the upstairs at Charlie's, right."

He put his hand on his bald head and stroked it for a long minute and said, "Why don't you just stick to investigating the murders. You're getting paid for that aren't you?"

"Sure, but I think there's a salable news piece on whatever is going on upstairs at Charlie's, and I have to look to the future."

"I'll tell you this much. If you want to have a future, stay away from the upstairs at Charlie's. That's all I'm going to say about it."

I left with a burning desire to know more about the upstairs. I may not be much of a detective, as Otto has suggested many times, but I can smell a news story and there was some kind of an odor coming from above at Charlie's. Maybe it was just a whore house, but I had to find out.

On the way back to my office, I waved to Maggie and grinned like a fool. She lifted her eyebrows, looked toward the ceiling. Her face reddened, but she smiled. I fed the cat, something I had forgotten again, and while it was eating I got a call from a local attorney, Ben Wilson, who wanted me to find out everything I could about a traffic accident. As usual, he didn't tell me which driver he represented. That way whatever information I gave him would be unbiased. We agreed that no matter how impartial a person tries to be he can be subconsciously influenced by a point of view.

He had been kind enough to point this out to me with specific examples in my own reporting. A nice guy, otherwise.

So I took care of the traffic business, all the time thinking about what I could do to discover who killed Linsley Sinclair and Harold

Hubbard. I decided to learn more about Linsley's history since she left high school. I knew about her association with Charlie and Harold. Was there more? I spent part of the afternoon talking to Linsley's mother after I called, and she accepted my offer to buy lunch. I joined her in eating salad at Hardee's.

Linsley was her only child, and she wanted to talk about her. I listened as she occasionally dabbed at her eyes. Nothing she said seemed pertinent to my investigation until she mentioned how unhappy Linsley was when she was going with Harold Hubbard.

"Why," I asked.

"I don't know exactly. I would ask her if she was so sick of going out with Harold why didn't she stop. She never really said, but she acted as though she couldn't quit, like she was afraid of him. He never seemed that threatening. They didn't come to the house much, once for dinner and maybe once or twice more."

She rambled on, and, when her voice wound down like a fading radio station, I said, "Do you suppose Hubbard had something on her. Something that he threatened to reveal unless she dated him?"

"What could it be?" Mrs. Sinclair said.

Yes, I thought, that's the question. What could it be?

On my way back to the office, I again grinned like a fool when I passed Maggie. She frowned before she looked away. Naturally, because of my lack of understanding of females, I was confused. The confusion increased when I found my office door wide open. I could have forgotten to lock it, of course. I wasn't that worried anyway. After all, what's to steal?

I entered cautiously and was greeted by a young woman sitting in my chair, bare feet on the desk, her hands behind her head.

"Hi, I'm Faustine," she said.

I leaned against the door frame and admired her definitely female parts and said, "I can see you are."

"Can the sex stuff, buddy. I'm here on business. Mister Randolph sent me."

"Did he tell you to break into my office and make yourself at home?"

"Break in. That's a laugh. My dead Aunt Sarah could pick that door lock."

"Really. Your dead Aunt Sarah?"

I was growing tired of this conversation, especially when it was apparent she was going to top anything I said.

"We'll operate like this," she announced.

I declared there would be no method of operation between us, and she could get her neatly packed butt off my chair. I didn't actually say "neatly packed."

She moved her feet to the floor slowly, stood up, and stretched. She came around to where I still was leaning against the door frame. Her auburn hair tickled my chin. She wiggled her hips and smiled. Her green eyes were highlighted by eye shadow. In an attempt to imitate Mae West, she said, "You will join me in a method of operation whether you want to or not, big boy."

She brushed past, leaving a heavy, intoxicating aroma and the feel of her body against mine.

I sat down in my still warm chair, tired from the encounter. She's not even pretty, I told myself. And she wasn't. She did have expressive eyes and that mass of shining hair, but her nose was as sharp as some cheese, and her mouth was too wide for her face.

Trying to remember how she was dressed, I visualized bare legs and arms. There was a remarkably short plaid skirt hugging her hips and a sleeveless blouse of some pale color. After wondering if she knew I wasn't a licensed private investigator, I decided I didn't care what she thought.

But I knew I cared what Maggie thought and began to suspect her frown was connected with Faustine. Just then Maggie tapped on the open door and entered.

"I see you have a new client. Is she old enough to be out of school at this hour?"

"It's past four o'clock," I said. "Let's go over to Otto's and forget about her."

"I just came up to remind you to feed the cat," Maggie said.

"Sure you did," I said to her back as she stomped out.

At Otto's I sat at the bar, sipped on a beer, and, between his waiting on customers we discussed women.

"I don't know why I'm talking to you about any of this, what do you know about women? There aren't any in your life, are there?" I said.

"Ya, you know I'm not that dumb. Not since my wife died. Not that I haven't had chances. Even a guy as old and worn out as me attracts women, especially old widows."

This apparently was a subject dear to his heart because he was unusually active in serving his customers and getting back to me.

"Ya, the trouble with women is that period thing. It just isn't natural. That's why they act so strange, are so unpredictable."

"You think women's periods are unnatural?"

"Well, does it seem right to you?"

"Otto, you must be kidding."

I knew he was, but I listened anyway.

"Hell no. Take this Maggie whatever. She gets mad at you, and you think it's because of this floozy PI she saw going up to your office. She won't even listen to an explanation. You know why? I'll tell you. She wants to make you miserable, that's why. Why? Because she is miserable. Ya, she either just had a period, is having one, or is mad because she knows she soon will have one."

I laughed and felt better, knowing at last that I now understood women.

CHAPTER NINE

The next day was a milestone of sorts. It was the beginning of my professional association with Faustine.

I felt half way decent when I went over to Otto's for the usual. I remembered to feed the cat and put the note I wrote to Maggie the night before under her office door.

In the note I explained how I understood her anger at me, using Otto's logic. I though maybe a laugh would help.

Faustine showed up before I finished my breakfast and before I had a chance to read about the Cubs' latest futile effort.

"Go away for at least another half hour. I'm reading. Git."

She didn't move from the bar stool next to mine. She ordered a cup of coffee and, "one of those." She pointed at the half-eaten doughnut near my cup.

"With a plate or napkin, something to put it on besides this bar," she told Otto.

I waited for Otto to make a caustic remark, but he just looked. She was quite a sight for that early in the morning.

Her hair was as glorious as I remembered, her nose as sharp, and her mouth as big but, somehow, in spite of the makeup, she looked young, vulnerable and sexy.

"Explain your theory about women to her," I said to Otto. "Incidentally Otto, this is Faustine, Faustine this is Otto."

"Faustine what," Otto asked as he spread a paper napkin in front of her and placed the doughnut on it with his pinkie extended.

When he returned with the coffee and placed it on a napkin she said, "Smith, my name is Faustine Smith."

She contorted her lips into an expression of disgust after she tasted the coffee but didn't comment. She nibbled at the doughnut, tapped it on the napkin like a person testing a hard boiled egg, and dropped it. If Otto heard the thud he pretended not to notice.

"Let's get down to business. Tell me what you know about these murders."

I thought of telling her to go to hell. I resented her being there to investigate what I already was investigating, like that little lawyer figured I wouldn't be able to handle it.

"How come Mister Randolph hired you? How old are you, anyway?"

"Why don't you call him and ask? I suppose he gave you his card. I'm twenty-eight. How old are you?"

We sparred for awhile longer, but eventually I told her everything I had learned so far, which, I realized, wasn't much. I didn't mention the upstairs at Charlie's.

"Do you have a copy of this sex book?"

When she wanted to see it and suggested we go to my office, I told her to finish her breakfast, and I would get it. I didn't want Maggie, who probably was in her office by then, to see me with Faustine.

When I brought the book back, opened to the pages like the ones at the murder scenes, complete with rubber bands holding the pages in place, she turned it over and read the title aloud.

"*Sex Etiquette: How to do it Right*, by Seymour Hares."

"Very funny," she said.

She wasn't laughing. I reminded her that she wanted to see it.

After studying the pages, she said, "You know about the drug that was used to kill these people, don't you."

"Sure," I said and attempted to pronounce the name of the stuff but wound up just saying "GHB."

"Do you know it's called 'the date rape drug,' and has it occurred to you there is some connection between the drug's use and this stupid book?"

"Of course it has," I said, "and I've been wondering who raped Hubbard."

"Maybe he did the raping," she said.

"Maybe he raped the Sinclair dame and somebody killed him because of that," Otto chimed in.

"Yeah, maybe, but why kill the Sinclair *dame*," Faustine said.

Otto retired to his cushioned chair and looked at the newspaper. The conversation was helpful. It reminded me of something I had planned to check on but had put off, figuring it was too far fetched.

"So, what do we do now?" Faustine said.

"We don't do anything. I told you, I work alone. Go do your nails or something."

I walked out of Otto's into the real world and headed for the police station. I stopped in a store doorway and looked back to see if Faustine was following. I didn't see her.

At the police station, I talked to Andy Brown about GHB and

where a person might get it. He said he figured it was probably like any other drug. Somebody was selling it, and people who wanted it knew who.

"Do you have anything new for me," Andy asked.

"Sluppleman's attorney has hired a young woman from Chicago, a PI, to investigate the case along with the rest of us."

"She was in here yesterday. I was thinking of arresting her for indecent exposure, but who knows what that is these days. She's something else."

At the courthouse, clerks greeted me like a long lost pain in the ass – good-naturedly of course – and turned me loose on the birth records for the same year Linsley Sinclair, Harold Hubbard, and the others graduated.

It took awhile. There was a lot of procreating going on in those days. I suppose there still is. I checked names against names, rechecked, thought for awhile, and checked again, but after a couple of hours I hadn't found a clue.

My eyes and head still ached when I got back to the office. Maggie was purposely, I thought, looking the other way when I passed, so I ignored her.

I left my office door open, turned on the radio, put my feet on the desk, and leaned back for a few minutes of rest before I began my weary journey again. In other words, I was stymied. What next?

The cat came into the room. Not caring if I scared it or not, I talked to it as though it was a member of the detective team, Bancroft & Cat. It didn't seem to mind. It even looked at me with its head cocked once as I talked and it explored.

"You know cat, if you could lower yourself to the point where you and I became friends, I would pet you and maybe even pick you up. Maybe Maggie would be impressed. What do you think?"

I put my feet on the floor, stood up, and watched to see if the cat ran. It didn't. I went to the door. When I turned the cat was in front of my desk watching. It showed no signs of panic.

I slowly closed the door. I opened it again. The cat moved to the side of the room when I returned to the desk. I discussed the case at length with my new partner, who, by then, was lying on the floor cleaning itself in a leisurely fashion.

Suddenly the cat was on its feet. It dashed out the door. A few seconds later Faustine appeared.

"What did you find at the courthouse? Why the interest in birth records for the year the murder victims graduated from high school?"

I didn't answer. She had followed me without my knowing it. Some gumshoe I was.

After waiting for me to answer, she said, "I talked to Doctor Sluppleman. He wants to talk to you. He knows something he isn't telling me, maybe he'll tell you."

"How long have you been in this business," I asked.

She thought about it for a moment and said, "About ten years now. I started with my uncle's agency when I was eighteen. My uncle is Fremont Randolph's brother."

She turned the guest chair, straddled it, rested her chin on its back, and looked into my eyes until I averted them.

"Why can't we work together," she said, still looking directly at me.

I put my elbows on the desk and leaned toward her. Our faces were a couple of feet apart. I stared into her eyes as she had mine. I was about to avert mine again when she blinked and looked away.

"What are you doing?" she stammered.

"Don't know what I'm doing," I sighed. "I'm lost in a sea of green, like the green of your eyes. Lost forever in a glorious dream that can never be."

She got up, paced the floor, and pointed a manicured finger at me.

"Can the bullshit and be serious. Randolph wants results, and I'm sure Sluppleman does too. Why won't you cooperate?"

"I'm a male chauvinist pig. I don't like playing second fiddle to a broad."

She threw up her hands, came back to the chair, turned it around, sat down, and crossed her legs. She fidgeted in the chair as silence engulfed us.

The cat came back into the room, cautious at first, but when Faustine murmured about what a pretty cat it was, it seemed to relax.

I was thinking of going bowling for awhile. Maybe, while I was trying to concentrate on bowling, an idea would sneak into my befuddled brain.

As I was wondering how I could get rid of Faustine, the cat came near her, appeared to listen to her talk, and rubbed its side against her leg. The ungrateful beast. It was purring and rubbing and appeared to be in cat heaven when Faustine reached to pet it.

The cat jumped back a few feet, arched its back, and hissed. Faustine pulled her hand back in mock fear and made soothing female sounds.

I was proud of my cat. It ignored her pitch and walked with an abundance of cat dignity out of the room.

"Is that your cat?"

"No way," I said. "It's a long story about a conniving female and a sucker who now is responsible for feeding the ungrateful thing," I said.

"Oh, I'll bet you mean the dish on the second floor, what's her name, Maggie?"

I ignored the question, told her I was going bowling, and that she should, as a responsible private investigator, earn her money by detecting. She claimed she needed time to think and would do it while she watched me bowl. After only a few frames, she was giving me bowling instructions.

"Think about it. You've already missed two seven pins. You're not giving yourself a chance. You need to move farther to the right to create more area and stroke the ball like you do on the other shots. You must be psyched out on that pin. Think of it as any other pin. You don't follow through when you shoot at it. Relax and let your hand follow the ball down the lane."

"Anything else," I said as I sat on the bench beside her.

"Yes. Relax your arm swing more on the first shot, follow through with your hand like I said, and you won't leave so many seven pins in the first place."

This conversation would have been amusing except she was correct. I had been told the same thing many times over the years by guys who know the game. To relax seemed to be something I couldn't do when it counted. There were times when my arm swing was as smooth as Faustine's thigh, but, when it counted, it often was sandpaper. It's called choking.

"You mean like this?" I said before I rolled the ball down the lane and neatly picked off the seven pin and left the other nine standing.

"It isn't that I can't do it right, it's just that I don't seem to be able to do it all the time. How do you know so much about bowling?"

"My brothers," she said. "We lived only a few blocks from Lovers' Lanes in Oak Park, and when they bowled, I had to tag along while our parents went out. My brothers tried to make a bowler out of me, and I got pretty good, I guess, but I hate the silly game."

I hated the "silly" game often enough myself, but to me it's like an unfaithful woman you can't resist.

It was a relief when Faustine told me she was going back to her motel. I told her I was going back to my office. After she was gone, I went to the police station and got permission to visit Doctor Sluppleman.

I was escorted to his cell. He was the top quest so he had a private one. He didn't look bad for a guy who had been in jail for awhile. I asked him how come his attorney couldn't get bail set, him being who he was.

"I should be out of here soon. A bail hearing is scheduled. Have you been able to learn anything that might help me?"

I admitted I was no where near finding all the answers. Later, as I left, he said, "Cheer up. This whole thing will be straightened out."

On my way back to the office, in front of the building, I ran into Harry Ballard, the guy for whom Maggie Atley worked.

It was one of few times I'd seen him since we were introduced. He's short, heavy with bushy eyebrows and hair growing out of his ears and nose. "Say Mister Ballard," I said, stopping him from hurrying away. "I hope my cat hasn't caused any problems in your office. I try to keep it upstairs, but sometimes, well you know how cats are."

I was hoping to make some points with Maggie by pretending the cat was mine.

"Yes," he said, "I know how cats are. I have three of my own. They're real characters. I didn't know there was a cat in the building. Don't worry about your cat, it won't bother me."

CHAPTER TEN

At Otto's, I slumped in a booth and stared at a half-empty glass of beer. Did Maggie lie about the cat just to make conversation? Or was there another reason?

She had been nosy. Just innocent interest? Playing to my ego by acting interested in my work? How did she know about me being at Charlie's? Did I tell her and not remember?

I shook my head, gulped the beer, and started to get up to get another. Faustine sat down across from me. For an instant, I wasn't sure it was her. Hair and eyes gave her away. She was wearing a loose fitting sweat shirt and jeans equally loose.

And her face. It was clean and fresh, like a washed apple. No makeup. She looked like a teen-ager.

"Before you buy me a beer, tell me what you have been thinking. I've been watching you."

"My thoughts are private. And I can't buy you a beer. You're too young."

She laughed and said, "I think that's a compliment. Buy me a beer."

After I purchased the beer, Otto came over to the booth and asked Faustine to see some identification. She said, "Thank you" and fished her driver's license out of a bag that looked as much like an oversized black jack as it did a purse. I wouldn't want her swinging it at me.

When Otto left I suggested that since we both had expense accounts, why didn't we go out to Charlie's restaurant and live it up a little.

"With me dressed like this?" she asked.

"I'm not exactly wearing a tux."

I was wearing my usual blue jeans, a T-shirt, and the ever-present Reeboks, the cleaner pair.

It took a little persuading, but she agreed, and, after finishing the beers we went to Charlie's and presented ourselves to the hostess, Ruth Romano-Laura Beckert.

It was Friday night, and there were more people in the place than I had seen before, but there still were many empty tables.

Ruth led us to a table in a back corner.

"That is one cool hostess," Faustine said. "She didn't even turn up her nose when she looked at us. Look. Now she's talking to that brute at the reservation desk. He looked back here once, quickly. I'll bet they're talking about us."

It was the same guy who had kept me from going upstairs before.

"You'll get used to being famous if you stick with me, baby," I said.

"It must be hell, you and your famous."

We were served beer in the tall, thin glasses and ordered steak with all the trimmings.

I watched the stairway to the second floor and counted the waitresses that went up. The number had reached five when Faustine said, "Are you going to let me in on whatever you're doing?"

I explained my interest in finding out what was happening on the second floor. She thought about it for awhile and said, "What does it have to do with the murders we're supposed to be investigating?"

"You never know," I said, not really believing there was a connection. But still, this was another opportunity to pursue what could be a money-producing story for me.

We ate and talked about the case.

"There isn't much to point at anyone except Doctor Sluppleman, is there?"

"Do you think he did it?" I asked.

She said she didn't have an opinion, that she was just interested in supplying Fremont Randolph all the information she could gather and get back to Chicago.

After we finished our meals, we lingered over drinks and endured long silences as I watched the stairway, and she watched me.

"Are we going to stay here forever?" she asked.

We paid our bills, left generous expense-account tips, and retired to the powder rooms. Later, when we had settled into my Escort, Faustine didn't protest when I said I wanted to stay and observe which cars remained after the place closed. She pushed the seat back and stretched out as far as her long legs would allow.

"How long will this take?"

I pushed my seat back and said, "Probably a couple of hours. They close in an hour. It'll take the customers awhile to clear out. I want to see who the people are that stay. Get the car license numbers. I've got a connection that will tell me who owns the cars."

"Gee, aren't you the efficient one," she said as she closed her eyes. She was snoring quietly soon after.

Stake outs are good for thinking if you can stay awake. I thought about Maggie. Somehow, in spite of a full stomach and heavy eyelids, I managed to stay awake. Finally, most of the cars were gone. Half-awake Faustine and I recorded the license plate numbers of those that remained.

We were back in the Escort ready to go when two men appeared at the sides of the car and yanked open the doors. The keys were in my pants pocket. Before I could get them, I was pulled from the car and patted down.

"Keep your hands off me, you goon," Faustine shouted.

I was pushed around to Faustine's side of the car and shoved against it. The guy who was doing the pushing on me was the big brute from the stairway. The other one I hadn't seem before.

"We're going for a walk," big brute said after he patted me down, his voice as menacing as a traffic accident. We were forced around to the back of the building where a bare light glowed weakly against the darkness. We were shoved through a door below the light. Inside, another light was turned on, revealing a small, windowless room. Two metal folding chairs, some clothes line rope, and two large cans that smelled of rotting garbage were in the room.

"Take off your clothes, all your clothes," big brute snarled.

If they had guns, they weren't showing.

"You'll never get away with this," I said. I swung at big brute. His forearm stopped the flight of my fist, and pain shot clear to my elbow.

"Don't get heroic, Nick. My dead Aunt Sarah is smarter than that," Faustine said. "I think we're out muscled. If they want to rape me and get AIDS let them go ahead."

"Don't flatter yourself lady," the other guy said. His voice was raspy, like his throat was lined with sand.

"Shut up," big brute growled.

Faustine pulled off her sweat shirt, a brassiere, and was dropping her jeans when big brute shoved me and said, "Get with it, or I'll rip your clothes off myself."

They threw our clothes in a corner of the room and demanded that we sit on the chairs facing each other. They tied our hands behind our backs and our ankles to the legs of the chairs.

Light from the bulb above cast shadows on Faustine's slender body, outlining the curves. I could hear the lock click as a key was turned in the door. Then the key was turned again, as if the door was being unlocked as quietly as possible. I tried not to look at Faustine, but we were so close.

We sat there staring at each other.

"I see you're rising to the occasion," Faustine said, looking directly into my eyes.

"Maybe, if we can turn the chairs around, we can untie each other," I said.

She started inching her chair around, and I did the same. Soon we were back to back. It was more difficult to move the chairs backward, but we managed until our hands touched.

She fumbled with the knots on the rope around my wrists but got nowhere. When she tired, I began working on the knots on her wrists. I was about to give up when I felt one of the loops loosen. In no time I had her hands free. She untied the ropes around her ankles and stood before me.

We had made some noise moving the chairs, but now there was silence as she knelt and untied my ankles. Then she stood up, still facing me, and reached around and tried to untie my hands. She smelled of soap. Little beads of sweat glistened on her skin. She moved around in back and finally got the knots loose.

I stood up, tested my knees. "What now?" she whispered.

It seemed warmer in the room. I stepped back and pointed to our clothes in the corner behind her. I noted the outline of vertebrae on her back as I followed her to the clothes. We dressed silently. I whispered that I thought they had just pretended to lock the door.

"Maybe this whole business was just to scare us," I whispered.

"It's working," she said. She pulled the sweat shirt over her head, still facing me. Her brassiere still was on the floor, and when I pointed to it, she picked it up and stuffed it into a back pocket. Most of it hung out like a workers' rag. I went to the door and turned the knob. The door opened. Light from the room probed the outside darkness beyond light cast by the outside bulb. Hand in hand we groped our way along the back wall of the building until we reached the parking lot side. My Escort sat where we left it, serene under the parking lot lights.

I wondered if all of this was just for entertainment. The goons, not ours. Maybe they would grab us again when we neared the car. But nothing happened. Starting the car shattered the silence, and it was all I could do to keep from burning rubber to get out of there. I imagined they were watching as they probably had been since leaving us in the room. I drove the Escort out of the parking lot at a leisurely pace. When we were on the road, Faustine allowed air to escape from her lungs and whispered, "Whee."

"I'm sorry I got you into this," I said.

"Those bastards sound and smell like Chicago organized crime to me. Unless you can show me that place has something to do with the murders, I'm staying the hell away. Why would they be trying to scare us?"

"The biggest one, the one who seems to be running the place, kept me from going upstairs one night. There must be something interesting going on up there. But I'll let it be for now."

I dropped Faustine off at her motel a block from the police station.

"Pleasant dreams," I said as I waited until she got to the door.

"More likely I'll have nightmares about you sitting in that chair in front of me expressing your deepest thoughts," she said.

I climbed the stairs to my office reluctantly. I was thinking I should have invited myself into Faustine's room, but as I went past Ballard's, an image of Maggie in my arms took over. The cat met me at the top of the stairs. It meowed and walked around in a small circle.

"I'll get your milk, don't fuss," I said.

When I turned toward the door, I saw that it was open. The lights were not on. After standing just outside the door and listening for a minute or so, I got up enough nerve to reach around and turn on the lights.

An examination from the doorway revealed there was no one there, but all the file drawers were open, and the contents were scattered on the floor. My guess was they were no longer in alphabetical order.

I checked the living quarters and found all my stuff still there. There was evidence that a search was made of the room, but nothing seemed damaged or missing.

The two goons from the restaurant? Had they tied us up so they could search my office?

A cold beer would have been welcome right about then. I poured the cat some milk and put the bowl in the middle of the room. I drank the rest of the milk from the bottle.

After it drank the milk, the cat explored the file folders and papers on the floor. It came around the desk and rubbed its side against my leg. I was sitting with my head on the desk, avoiding the task of putting the files back in order, and wondering what could have been in them that interested anyone.

Jackson's file on Charlie's, of course. I got down on my knees and began searching. Once I had the folders together, it was obvious the one marked "Charlie's" was missing.

I had something to worry about. Whoever wanted that file was not going to believe all it included was a large question mark. They would probably beat the hell out of me, maybe kill me before they were convinced I hadn't hidden the rest of the file somewhere else.

The cat was curious. I pushed it aside gently and with caution for fear of being clawed. As I sat leaning against the file cabinet, dreading sorting the papers and getting them back in the proper folders, the cat walked onto my lap and sat down.

I moved my hand cautiously toward it, ready to withdraw if it objected. The purring continued. I petted the cat on its head and wondered what I was getting myself into, not only with the case and the business at Charlie's, but with the cat ... and Maggie. I had to show her how I domesticated her cat. Or was it domesticating me?

CHAPTER ELEVEN

It was a little after ten the next morning when I went over to Otto's and saw Faustine reading the sports pages of the local paper. I complained that the pages were mine by reason of longevity. She shoved them toward me on the bar and said with disgust, "The Cubs lost again."

"Thanks a lot," I said. "You've ruined the suspense."

Otto laid the local section of the paper in front of us and opened it to page six. I spotted the one-column photo of my mug immediately and saw a headline that said, "Local cleanup campaign started."

It was a short piece about the alley cleanup with several quotes from Commissioner Gordon. BJ and I were named but the three teenagers were not.

"What's this about?" Otto demanded.

"Just part of my campaign to get people to recognize and do something about their civic duty. Our next project is to clean up this dump," I said.

"I'm all for that," Faustine said.

Otto grumbled that I would tell him what's going on sooner or later. Faustine stared at me.

"What do you plan to do today, Mister Civic Duty?"

"I'm going to call Doctor Sluppleman. He's been released on $500,000 bond. I hope you can think of something to do besides tag along like a little sister. Did you have nightmares?

"Once I realized what a small threat you are, I slept fine, thank you."

Otto, as usual, was listening to the conversation although he would deny it. I was glad he didn't understand the innuendo.

"Why is it you, with ten years of experience in this business, are always tagging along after me? Were you hired to keep an eye on me, or are you just unable to do any detecting on your own?"

She choked on coffee she had just swallowed and stood up, glaring at me.

"If I was hired to watch you, I've seen all there is to see. Jam it mister."

She marched out, her menacing bag swinging from her shoulder.

Otto looked at me for an explanation. I shrugged and said, "You tell me. You're the one who thinks he understands women."

When I called Sluppleman, who had returned to his practice in Chicago, he asked in a subdued voice, "Have you learned anything that will help clear me?"

I admitted my failure, so far, to learn much of anything that would help. He said I should be careful.

"And warn Charlie Connor to be careful."

"What about Laura Beckert? Shouldn't I warn her, too?"

He agreed and repeated that I should be careful. He told me to keep at it and asked me to cooperate with his attorney's investigator.

"Did Fremont send you a retainer fee yet? Was $2,000 enough?"

I assured him it was and, after he hung up, opened the mail I had neglected for two days.

I found the check among bills and junk mail. I went to my bank, a branch of United Fed up the hill from the police station, and deposited the check. I gloated at the balance in my check book.

Meanwhile, the names connected to the license plate numbers Faustine and I recorded at Charlie's turned out to be interesting.

The plates all belonged to politicians. The name that interested me most was Powell Brewster, our local state representative. One of the others was a state senator and another was a state representative from another district.

I decided to visit Charlie again at the golf course, hoping to catch him when he was stupid from drink and would talk freely. I also wanted to send to the goons the message that they hadn't scared me off. What a brave fellow I was. And stupid. Faustine's dead Aunt Sarah would have had more sense.

I sipped a beer at the golf course clubhouse waiting for Charlie to finish his round. I felt guilty for violating Otto's rule about no beer before four o'clock. Several groups of golfers sat around tables drinking and telling lies.

My beer was nearly gone, the bartender had asked me twice if I wanted a refill, when Charlie came in with three other guys.

Apparently he had been drinking while he played because his eyes were red, and he seemed silly-happy. One of the guys in the group was Powell Brewster. I recognized him because I interviewed him once when I worked for the newspaper and had, of course, seen his face in many a campaign ad.

He looked like a model in a men's magazine ad for expensive clothes. His hair was sandy and fluffed on top to make him look taller. It covered his ears. His eyebrows were the same color as his hair, and I believe they were plucked. Honest. In spite of the sun it must have been exposed to because of the golf, his skin was pale, translucent.

Somehow he still was in office. One of his most recent transgressions, according to what I had heard, was the purchase of hugely expensive personal office furniture at the state's expense. I don't remember the figure, but it was beyond what anyone but a crook would spend, especially when it wasn't his money. Or, at least, it wasn't supposed to be.

After the group ordered drinks, Charlie proposed a toast. No one paid any attention. One of the guys was busy with the scorecard, and Powell Brewster was busy pruning himself.

Charlie saw me.

"Hey, Nick," he shouted, "did you find Laura Beckert?"

He laughed and beckoned me to join them. I did. There were introductions. Two of the names were meaningless to me, and their owners were no more interested in me than I in them. But Powell Brewster gave me his politically correct greeting and perked up even more when Charlie said I was a reporter for the local newspaper.

"Used to be," I corrected Charlie.

That didn't seem to matter to Representative Brewster. He already was into explaining what a wonderful job he was doing for the people of his district and how pleased he was to meet me.

I cringed and thought of mentioning furniture to stop the flow of bullshit. Instead, I mentioned Charlie's restaurant and how I enjoyed the food the night before.

"I suppose you did too, sir," I said.

"What do you mean?"

"Perhaps I was mistaken. I thought I saw you there."

It didn't seem possible that his face would turn paler, but it did. His eyes darted around like those of a cornered animal. Before Brewster could blurt out whatever he was trying to say, I turned to Charlie and said I had indeed found Laura Beckert.

"Her dad was pleased," I added.

The silly smile vanished from Charlie's face. He looked just as much a trapped skunk as did Brewster. Why?

"What do you mean, her dad? The old man's in Florida, isn't he?"

"Yes," I said, enjoying his confusion and not offering anything to ease it. This was a new angle. What did Charlie fear from Beckert?

Brewster interrupted.

"I don't know why you think I was at Charlie's last night, or any time for that matter," he said.

"Is it important?"

He considered this for a moment and sighed.

"Just a case of mistaken identity I suppose. I was not there."

I stood and said, "Nice to have met you gentlemen. I have to leave. Have an appointment with Detective Andy Brown."

I didn't see any point in staying. Maybe I could catch Charlie alone at another time. I didn't have an appointment with Brown, but I drove to the police station because I wanted to tell him what had been going on with me and, maybe, get some new information from him.

He wasn't in. I left a message asking him to call and went back to the office. I was pleasantly surprised when Maggie smiled at me as I went by. When I opened my office door, there was a note on the floor. It was from her. In it she said she had to talk to me, and that the nonsense about female periods was stupid.

"There is nothing funny about periods!" the note stated.

As usual, I left the office door open and was pondering Maggie's note when the cat announced its presence by making "I-want-some-milk" noises. I poured the milk and watched the cat while hoping Brown would call soon so I could get over to Otto's and surround a beer.

The cat startled me when it jumped from the floor to the top of the desk. It walked around the edges, checked the middle, and sat down in front of me.

I moved my hand slowly toward its head, still leery of the possibility of being clawed. It sat contentedly as I stroked the fur on its head and neck.

Maggie tapped on the door and said, "May I come in."

The cat leaped half way across the room and flashed past her legs before I could answer. She came in and smiled.

"I see you and Ruffles have become friends."

"Yeah," I said. "Me and the cat Mister Ballard doesn't want around."

She sat down and was silent for a moment. She apologized for avoiding me. According to her, she had not intended to get so emotionally involved. She thought, she said, that she could have a little fling, like her husband, and forget it.

"I lied about the cat just so I'd have reason to talk to you."

"Your husband?"

"Yes. I'm married and have two boys. They both are in college. My husband and I are separated. He's living with one of his floozies. We've been separated for nearly a year. You know how it is."

Did I? Know how it is. For instance, I knew she lied to me about Ballard and the cat, and for all I knew she was lying now.

"I'm sorry," she said, breaking the silence.

The phone rang. It was Brown. I told him I would call him back. He said he was going home, and, if I called him there, he would arrest me. I agreed to see him first thing in the morning.

Maggie stood and said she had to go, refusing my offer to buy her a drink and discuss our situation further. We left the building together. Did I care that she was married? It never had occurred to me. She wasn't wearing a ring. I didn't want to get too involved anyway, I told myself.

As I mulled over such thoughts and drank a beer in my favorite booth at Otto's, BJ came in, stood at the doorway for a moment, and spotted me. He came back to the booth and asked if it was all right if he sat down. I bought him a Coke, returned to my seat, and waited.

"Mister, do you think it would be all right if I cleaned up Hellerman Park?"

Before I could answer, the three guys who had helped clean up the alley were there, towering over us. They were pissed because they didn't get any credit for helping clean up the alley. I explained, as if I were talking to infants, that if they refused to tell me their names...

"The story wasn't my idea anyway. It was Gordon's. He couldn't pass up the chance for favorable publicity."

Two of the guys pushed into the booth and sat down. The third one, the littlest, got a chair, and straddled it.

BJ repeated his plan to clean up the block-square park, "If it's all right."

After being prodded, I bought sodas for each of them, and we sat "in committee" discussing JB's plan.

"The drug guys control that park. That's where they make a lot of their sales. None of the parents who care will let their kids play there," the biggest guy said.

I gradually gained enthusiasm for the project in spite of the danger. I was sure I could sell a story with "before and after" photos to a Chicago newspaper. Cleanup projects make salable copy. But the bastards who took the little park away from the kids wouldn't appreciate our being there.

"I may be able to get police protection while we clean the place and maybe for the kids to use it later, but I'm not going to do anything until I know who you guys are."

BJ hummed while they mumbled among themselves.

The biggest guy said, "I'm Jack Horner. They call me Little Jack. I stifled a laugh. His glare warned me not to comment. The littlest guy said his name was James Bradley and the third guy said, "I'm Dino Mancuso, everybody calls me Lump."

So it was Little Jack, James, and Lump. BJ's lips moved as he repeated the names to himself.

I agreed to talk to the police department about getting protection and to let them know as soon as I could. They were just leaving as Faustine came in. She pretended she didn't see me and sat at the bar, ordered a gin and tonic.

After a brief conversation with Otto, she headed for the potty, ignoring me as she went by. She was wearing auburn shorts, auburn sandals, and a white blouse with an auburn breast pocket. All of the auburn was the same shade as her hair. Every bleary eye in the joint was on her as she moved.

I picked up her drink from the bar. Otto said he had a policy against patrons stealing drinks, and I told him to mind his own business. After putting the drink on the edge of the booth where she couldn't miss it when she returned, I sat and waited.

She came past, scooped the drink from the booth, and returned to the bar. Otto grinned.

I finished my beer and walked past the bar on my way out. Faustine turned just as I was about to pass and put her thigh in my path. I could have gone around, but I stood there, thigh to thigh, and waited.

"Let's go back to the booth and talk about things of mutual interest. I'm sorry I let my annoyance with your stupid attitude interfere with business."

Otto grinned.

When she sat down across from me, I waved to Otto and ordered another beer. He made an obscene gesture with a finger.

"Want another drink," I asked Faustine, and when she said she did, I was stuck with buying her one as well as a beer for myself.

"I've been working all day," she said, and when I made the mistake of asking what she had been doing she started talking.

She gave me details, lots of details, about her leg work while trying to learn where a person could buy GHB. She explained how she showed photos from the high school yearbook to the few drug

72

dealers she found.

"How did you get a copy of the yearbook?"

"I borrowed yours. I knew you wouldn't mind. I'll give it back. The point is, we aren't going to find out anything from the dealers. They say there are so many customers they don't remember most of them. Guys buy the stuff and woman and girls buy it.

And so we sat there, drinking and talking.

We went to eat at Lou's Restaurant around the corner from Otto's. We had drinks with our meal and a couple more after we finished.

I was enjoying having someone to talk to besides Otto, and when Faustine indicated she was going back to her motel, I said I would tag along.

"*We* are not going any place, lover boy. I'm going back to my motel and sleep so I can get my ass to working on what Randolph told me to do tomorrow."

"Randolph? Oh yeah, Sluppleman's attorney. What does he want you to do?"

"What I should have done in the first place, find out every detail I can of what Sluppleman did the night Linsley Sinclair was murdered and maybe some details of what he did the night this other guy was murdered. Maybe he has alibis for both nights. Alibis he doesn't know he has."

After she made me promise I wouldn't try to worm my way into her motel room, she agreed to let me walk her back to the place. I apparently was getting a little silly from the drink because I wanted to hold her hand while we walked.

"Oh no," she said. "I've been down that road before. You scratch my palm with a finger nail, sending chills up my spine and elsewhere, and the next thing you know... "

So I walked her back to her room, tried to kiss her, and backed off when she reminded me of my promise. I went back to Otto's for a nightcap.

He grinned when I came in. It wouldn't have been half as annoying if he had said something, but he just grinned, apparently aware, because of the time, that I had struck out.

CHAPTER TWELVE

The next day, while Faustine was doing her thing, I called Sluppleman and asked him where he was the nights Linsley Sinclair and Harold Hubbard were killed.

He said he stayed at the Holiday Inn and spent both nights studying new developments in psychiatry.

I reported I still hadn't found any evidence that would clear him. He said, "I have every confidence in Fremont Randolph. And you. Between the two of you, I'm sure we'll clear this matter up."

He said he had patients waiting and hung up.

I fed the cat. Now I was feeding it near the desk.

I talked over the problems of the investigation with it for awhile. The cat didn't offer any advice. It was too busy preening itself. Later I closed the door, leaving it in the office, and headed over to Otto's for breakfast.

Maggie was just unlocking her office door when I descended the stairs from the third floor. I informed her that the name "Ruffles" was not exactly appropriate for the cat that was hanging around my office, and, if it had to have a name, it should be "Tom."

"You're sure?"

"I'm sure," I said.

At Otto's, I stared at the sports pages without seeing. I decided to check with the desk clerk at the Holiday Inn to see if Sluppleman stayed in all night.

Otto got up from his chair and snapped his fingers in front of my face.

"Are you in a trance?"

"I'm depressed," I said. "Don't mess with me, I might be dangerous."

"What else is new? Aren't you always depressed when the ladies put you in your place? I like this Faustine."

"Instead of helping my client, I'm thinking of checking out his story. Some detective."

"Ya, well, isn't that part of any investigation, especially when there is a pending trial? His attorney has to know if he is telling the truth, otherwise how can he defend him?"

I agreed but still didn't know what I could do for the rest of the day to earn my money. I was going to the police station to see Brown but, I didn't expect much from that.

Faustine came in, sat, and said, "I've got some news."

Otto poured her a cup of coffee, placed a doughnut on a napkin in front of her, and stood waiting for the news.

"Should I be talking in front of ... well, you know what I mean."

I assured her there was no need to fear talking in front of Otto.

"He's so old he won't remember what you said long enough to tell anyone else."

Otto returned to his chair and pretended to be reading the newspaper.

"You know that goon, the big one who seemed to be the boss at Charlie's, the one who insisted we take off our clothes, the one who helped tie us to the chairs?"

If a human's ears could perk up like a dog's, I'm sure Otto's would have. Faustine had his attention.

She leaned toward me and whispered, "His name is Tony Carbrunda. He's a member of Chicago organized crime."

"No kidding," I said loud enough for Otto to hear.

She leaned toward me again and whispered, "Ramsey Sinclair is a mob attorney."

I thought all of this was just a performance for Otto's benefit and repeated, "No kidding."

"Listen, you jerk, what I'm telling you is the truth. I've got sources in Chicago. There's no doubt about the information."

She was no longer whispering. I continued to question her information without revealing what it was. She convinced me it was true. Otto, I was sure, heard all of the conversation except the whispered part.

His attempt to pretend he was not interested amused me until I began considering the danger involved in sticking my nose into the restaurant's business. And I had tried to make sure they knew I wasn't frightened away. Great.

Faustine left without saying where she was going. I didn't have the nerve to ask.

On the way to the police station to talk to Brown, I checked to see if anyone was following. I felt silly, knowing Faustine had been able to follow me without me seeing her, but I was nervous.

What if some hit man from Chicago was on my tail?

I made it to the police station alive and must have looked worried because Brown asked me if some woman's husband was after me. I thought of Maggie, but it wasn't her husband, whoever he was, that worried me. Brown rapped his hand on the desk and said, "Come out of it Bancroft, where ever you are. I'm a busy man."

"I suppose you knew that guy who appears to be running Charlie's, Tony Carbrunda, is a mobster from Chicago, and that Ramsey Sinclair is a mob attorney."

"You are a detective, aren't you," Brown said, not sparing the sarcasm.

He said, "What difference does it make to you? You are staying away from that story you think is there, right? I warned you, remember."

"Is the police department being bought off," I asked, revealing my lack of common sense at the moment. You don't accuse a policeman of being on a crook's payroll and expect him to continue giving you information.

"You believe that if you must. Just stay away from the place, or you'll screw everything up and get yourself killed."

The anger in his voice warned me not to tell him about the little room and the chairs.

"What about the murders? Do you have anything new you can tell me?"

"Right now, I'd rather tell the murderer than you," he said. "Get out of here and come back next Spring."

I left, hoping I hadn't permanently loused up our relationship. I spent some time at the bowling lanes halfheartedly practicing and mostly trying to think. I decided to go to Laura Beckert's apartment and see if she was there and would talk to me. It was a surprise when she answered after the first ring.

"Charlie, get the hell out of here. I just woke up. I told you to get out of my life, and I mean it this time. Go rape one of those bimbos at the golf course."

As I digested this information she shouted, "Well."

"My name is Nick Bancroft. I'd like to talk to you some more about the murders. I talked to you before, but I'm working for a new client who needs help."

"Come on up if you want, but I'm not getting dressed, and I'm making some coffee before I talk to you or anybody else."

She buzzed me into the building. I went up to the second floor. The door to her apartment was open. I walked in and closed it, hoping the noise would alert her to the fact that I was inside.

She walked out of the kitchen and casually wrapped the open silk robe around her after she entered the living room.

"Sit down," she said, indicating a couch fronted by a coffee table. She sat next to me, causing the cushions to sink even further. It was like sitting on a waterbed.

She crossed her legs, sighed, and leaned back. The robe, pink flowers on a black background, slid off to each side. She made no effort to put it back.

They were good, those legs. Slender, shaved, and tanned. I wanted to turn and look at her face, but the cushions on the couch were so soft I didn't risk it.

"The coffee will be done in a moment. You want some and maybe a Danish, if I have any?"

She got up, stretched, and said, "Let's sit at the kitchen table. It's more comfortable than this damned thing. Imagine trying to make out on this couch. It's not the greatest, I can tell you."

I imagined it as we walked to the kitchen and sat across from each other on dinette chairs.

She put her head in her hands and said, "I feel like hell, and I must look that way."

Without saying so, I agreed. Her face was lean, unlike the rounded innocence I saw in the high school yearbook. Her eyes were sunken and red. She would be attractive, in spite of the hard edges, if she had adequate rest and combed her hair, I decided.

The coffee pot stopped gurgling. She got up and poured, looked at the cups, gave me the one that wasn't chipped, and said, "Well."

"You have a nice place here."

Even the kitchen was large. The living room wall facing the lake was mostly glass and presented a view of lawn sloping toward the water. Geese combed the lawn for food and, I imagine, shit all over the place. Good for the grass. I could see she was getting agitated because I didn't get on with the questioning. Normally I would have let her stew, hoping it would cause her to reveal more than she intended, if she had anything besides her body to reveal.

However, this time it didn't seem wise to mess with her mind. She looked like an explosion about to happen. Her hands were shaking as she lit a cigarette.

"Doctor Sluppleman is in trouble. They found one of his pens at the scene of Linsley's murder, and his finger prints were on a book found on Hubbard's lap after he was murdered."

"I read about that," she said as she snuffed out the cigarette in a saucer.

"Poor Sluppleman. The worm has turned and turned again. He was the high school joke, and then he made us all look like jokes with his fancy office and expensive fees. He thinks he knows more about what people feel and think than God. And now he's humble again, I'll bet, as he faces a murder charge. Why do you suppose he did it?"

When I suggested that maybe he didn't, that it looked like someone was trying to frame him, she stood up and walked into the living room. I followed. She paced back and forth in front of the window. The light outlined her body inside the robe.

It was disconcerting, but I slogged on.

"Are you a patient of his?"

"What! What makes you think I'm a patient of his or any other shrink? Who needs a shrink? Do I look like I'm crazy?"

I explained that when I was trying to find her and was watching her apartment, I saw Doctor Sluppleman there, also trying to find her.

"It was just business. We have a business arrangement."

"What kind of business?"

"Do I have to spell it out for you? I'm a professional. A prostitute. He is one of my customers, but if you blab that, I'll deny it."

"Have the police talked to you," I asked.

"Of course they have. They gave me a bunch of shit about not being home right after the murder. They shut up when I told them who I was with. I asked them to go ahead and call the guy, but I doubt they had the nerve."

"Who was it?"

"I'm not telling you. It's a private matter. The police must be satisfied. I haven't heard from them."

"Were you at work, I mean the restaurant, on the nights Linsley and Hubbard were murdered?"

She stopped her pacing and faced me.

"Why don't you ask Tony?"

I pretended ignorance about Tony, but she sneered and said, "You know Tony, the big bastard who runs Charlie's. Sure you know him."

She said she was going to take a shower, and I might as well go because she wasn't going to answer any more questions.

As she headed for the bedroom, and, I assume, the shower, she let the robe slide from her shoulders. It tumbled onto the pale blue carpet after hesitating at her hips. She turned at the doorway and said, "Why do men find a woman's body so fascinating? I'm sure you watched all the way. Surely you've seen a naked woman before. Why are you so interested?"

"I think it has something to do with sex," I said.

She was peeking around the doorway now, everything but her

face hidden. She was being coy. I found myself wondering how much she charged. I didn't ask. Instead, I left with images of sugar plums dancing in my head. I guess they weren't sugar plums, exactly, but close enough.

On my way back to the office, Maggie smiled at me. I ignored her. I was trying to get up enough nerve to call Brown and ask if Laura Beckert had an alibi and, if so, who confirmed it.

The cat didn't appear to be in the office. My living quarter's door was shut so I wondered, briefly, where it was. Must have its own way in and out, I decided.

I jacked up my courage and called Brown.

"Look Andy, I'm sorry about..."

He didn't let me finish but insisted that I get to the point because, "I'm a busy man."

"Did Laura Beckert's alibi work out? She indicated she was with some big shot but wouldn't tell me his name."

"I'm not going to tell you his name either. He denies even knowing her. Naturally he would. Her alibi is no better than yours."

He hung up before I could say anything more.

The cat wandered into the room. I didn't see where it entered. Maybe it could walk through walls. It wanted milk. As I was feeding it, the phone rang. It was Maggie asking if she could come up for a couple of hours after work.

"Do you want to see the cat?"

"You know what I want. May I come up or not?"

I pretended to be hurt because she only wanted to see me when she wanted *that*. Actually, it did bother me a little. I reminded myself to be careful what I told her.

When she arrived, the cat was sitting on my desk as I stroked its head. It was making those contented sounds and didn't run when Maggie appeared.

"I see you can even charm a wayward cat," she said as she approached the desk. The cat made a soft thud as it landed on the floor. It went to a corner, sat, and looked watched.

CHAPTER THIRTEEN

Four hours later, Maggie left. I stretched like a contented cat. After taking a shower, I went to Lou's restaurant to eat. I took my time getting around the hot beef, drank a second bottle of beer, and didn't get to Otto's until about ten o'clock.

"Faustine gave up waiting for you. Call her. Says it is important," Otto said.

I leaned my head against my hand with my elbow on the bar and drew little circles with a finger. I wasn't doing it to annoy Otto. I was thinking of Maggie.

"OK, so don't talk to me. I don't know why Faustine wants to talk to you; you don't have anything to report anyway."

"Nothing to report," I agreed.

Otto accused me of being on drugs, waited on a couple of customers, put a glass of beer in front of me, and retired to his chair.

The beer was warm by the time I finished it, and still I sat there. Otto was about to pour another glass when I said, "If that's for me, forget it. I've got to go in a minute."

He put the glass down, looked at me as though I was about to vomit on his bar, and said, "Well, aren't you going to call her?"

"Who?"

He mumbled something under his breath, sat down, and said, "If you are on drugs get out of here. I don't serve junkies."

I waved to him with a limp wrist, got up, and left. I wasn't as completely out of it as I made it appear. Still, I was in a state of contentment rare to me. I hummed to myself as I walked the few blocks to the Holiday Inn.

There was something about a motel lobby that attracted me. Strangers, coming and going. I watched and wondered who they were and why they were there. I sat on a couch as if I had nothing better to do. Besides, the clerk at the reception desk was busy answering the phone and waiting on customers even at this late hour.

She was about thirty years old, had short straight hair and inquisitive brown eyes. When she was free, I approached and placed the newspaper photo of Sluppleman in front of her. She looked at it and said, "It's a photo of Doctor Sluppleman, so..."

"You know him, then."

"Who are you?" she asked, politely but with an attitude that told me she didn't give out information about guests.

I explained that I was investigating a murder and was trying to clear him of it. She insisted on seeing some identification and was suspicious when I couldn't display a private investigator license.

"I answered police questions about Doctor Sluppleman. He's a guest here often."

After a few rounds of give and take, she decided to cooperate. She said Doctor Sluppleman was a guest on the nights in question.

"Did you see him after, say, eight o'clock on the night of the murder of Linsley Sinclair?"

"I already told police so I guess it won't hurt to tell you. He left about eleven o'clock that night. I remember because he had a red rose in his lapel. He took it off and gave it to me. I guess it was left over from the convention of psychiatrists. He was the main speaker. A nice man, after you get over the way he looks at you, right into your eyes; know what I mean?"

"What time did he come back?"

She shrugged her shoulders and said, "Maybe after I got off work at one. I didn't see him."

The phone rang; she answered it and held the receiver away from her ear. She raised her eyebrows and held the phone so I could hear a woman talking."

She put her hand over the receiver and said, "She is a regular. Wants to talk most every night about this time. It will be awhile."

I nodded and left. I should have stayed and asked her what she knew of Sluppleman the night Hubbard was killed.

I still was tired, a nice comforting tiredness, and was looking forward to a long sleep. It occurred to me that I would have to straighten up the bed a little. When I opened the office door and turned on the light, the cat raced up to me and began meowing and rubbing itself against my leg. It seemed agitated. I was annoyed. It was getting to be a pain in the ass.

It kept nudging against my leg, and, just as I tripped over it, a blast of what I thought was fire came from the doorway of my dark living quarters.

I fell from the force of something smashing into my right arm just above the elbow. Shocking pain drew my left hand to the area. I felt something sticky. Blood, warm blood, my blood! There was another flash from the darkness. Then the noise of someone moving. I thought the gunman was coming to shoot me again. I curled up, hiding my face under my good arm, and waited for the worse.

I heard the sound of pounding feet coming from outside and then down the stairway. Whoever had shot at me was getting away. I continued to lie there, still in a ball, when the cat rubbed against my face, making purring noises.

I got up, sat at my desk for a few minutes holding my wounded arm. I called police and told the woman dispatcher I had been shot. She took my address, told me to stay put, and said she was sending an ambulance.

Maybe I passed out because the next thing I remember is being in the hospital emergency room. My arm was being bandaged. Later a young policeman I didn't know was recording all the information I gave in a notebook.

It took awhile, what with all the paperwork, but I finally got out of there. The young cop drove me back to my office. He talked about all the violence in the world and how too much of it was right around us all the time. I had no trouble agreeing.

As I lay in bed trying to sleep, my arm ached even though, as the cowboys used to say, it only was a flesh wound. No matter what position I assumed, it hurt.

My mind raced as I tried to figure out who shot me and the reason why. Probably someone connected with the two goons at Charlie's restaurant. But why? Did they think I knew more than I did? And the gunman must have been a professional if he was working for them. Would he have left me there alive? Did he think his shots had been fatal? And when it was revealed that I still was alive, would he try again?

I suppose I managed to sleep some, but when I got up and turned on the radio the next morning, my arm still ached dully, and I felt as dragged out as a one-legged distance runner.

The shooting was mentioned on the radio newscast. The wound was described as more serious than it was. Brown called and said he wanted me to come to his office as soon as possible.

"So, now you want to talk to me," I said.

"You're damned right I want to talk to you. Get here as soon as you can, or I'll have you picked up."

Apparently he was pissed off at me for getting shot. I'll have to try to avoid that in the future.

I would go to the police station all right, but first I was going to have a cup of coffee and a doughnut at Otto's.

It was difficult getting a shirt on. The wound bled a little, but I managed to soak up the smear of blood before I struggled into a shirt and pants. Tying my shoelaces was an adventure.

When I sat down at the bar, Otto said, "What the hell are you doing here. Shouldn't you be in bed?"

"It was only a flesh wound, partner. I'm gonna have me some coffee, and then I'll saddle up and go after them varmints."

"How many were there?"

"It was dark, maybe a dozen."

"Ya, sure, a dozen."

Otto poured coffee and placed a doughnut on a napkin. The napkin had become a staple since Faustine arrived. The coffee actually tasted good. And I was hungry. I ate the doughnut and asked for another.

"Not until you to tell me what happened."

"When Faustine gets here, I'll tell you down to the last detail. Why tell you now when I'll just have to repeat it when she arrives?"

We argued about whether she would arrive or not and what harm there would be if I had to repeat the story.

"I may decide to write a book about this caper and not tell anyone until the book comes out," I said.

Otto tossed me a doughnut, grumbled, gave me the sports pages of his newspaper and said the shooting wasn't even in the paper, as far as he could see. He said he heard it on the radio.

"It happened too late for the newspaper. They might mention it in tomorrow's edition."

I was reading about the latest Chicago Cub disaster when Faustine came in, sat down, and said, "I hear you've been shot."

"I hear you wanted me to call you," I said.

"It turned out to be nothing. Tell me about being shot. Why aren't you in the hospital or at least in bed?"

"It was only a flesh wound," Otto snorted.

So I told them the details, trying in my modesty not to describe too much. Like when I curled up in a ball waiting to die.

Faustine had to examine the bandage and appeared to be impressed when she saw the dried blood on it. We talked about who the shooter might have been.

When I could put it off no longer, I announced my intention of reporting to Brown at the police station. Faustine insisted on accompanying me.

"You know, don't you, that we are in deep water here. There's something going on out at that restaurant, and, whatever it is, they think it's worth protecting. They are telling you, us, in no uncertain terms to stay the hell away," Faustine said.

"It seems that way," I replied.

Outside Brown's office, I sat on a bench and waited while he talked on the phone, left the office, and came back maybe ten minutes later.

"So there were two shots fired," he said when he got back. "We want to examine your office. Dig out the bullets if we can find them. We'll get a search warrant if we have to."

"You don't need a search warrant. Just break in like everyone else does. The lock is as easy to pick as your nose apparently."

"I'm thinking this has something to do with Charlie's. I told you to stay away from there. My job is seldom easy, but it becomes a pain in the ass when I have to beg jerks like you to stay away."

"I've got a job, too. You think I like begging assholes like you for information that belongs to the public, not the police force."

"OK, OK, let's start over. Do you have any idea who shot you?"

I explained that I didn't and described the whole thing as he looked at notes, apparently the ones supplied by the young cop.

"I'm sorry I had the poor taste to get shot," I said.

"Mind your own business, and maybe, just maybe, you won't be shot again."

"You know the answer to that. My business is reporting. There's a story out there at Charlie's, a story worth some money to me, I think, and I'm going to get it."

"I guess you aren't satisfied with the money from investigating the two murders, then."

We had settled down to talking instead of shouting, and I asked him if he had anything new on the murder investigations.

"What do you have?"

I admitted I had nothing. I did have a theory I wasn't ready to discuss.

"When I'm sure you can keep your nose out of what's going on at Charlie's, at least for now, I'll think about feeding you some information on the murders."

I stood up to leave and said, "I guess that means you don't have anything new either."

"Think what you want," he said, "and try to stop making work for us by getting shot."

With friends like that, how could I think of leaving the business? Maybe I'll even get a private investigator's license and a permit to carry a gun.

After joining Faustine outside the station, I admitted I was tired, and said I was going back to my living quarters to rest, maybe even go back to bed.

She insisted on getting some bandaging material as we passed a drugstore. She wanted to play nurse and change the dressing on my arm. In my room, as she fussed around applying a new bandage, I asked her again why she wanted me to call her the night before.

"It was nothing, just forget it," she said.

"Otto said it was important, that you said it was important. What was it?"

"If you must know, I wanted you to come to my motel room and ... don't worry about it. The feeling passed."

Only the snipping of a pair of scissors as she trimmed the bandage broke the silence.

"There," she said. "A fine bandage, even if I do say so myself."

She gathered the trimmings, the sack the stuff came in, and put it all in a waste basket, one that needed emptying.

"I've got to get more rest. Thanks for the bandage. When I get up, I'm going to find out what Linsley Sinclair was doing the night she was murdered. If she was with anyone, if anyone saw her, that kind of stuff.

"I would have done this before, but I thought Brown would tell me. Now he won't tell me much of anything."

I said, "Why don't you try to get the same kind of information on Harold Hubbard. We could meet at Otto's later and compare notes."

She thanked me with her eyes for not saying anything more about the call she wanted me to make and agreed to inquire about Hubbard.

After she left, I put out food for the cat and called the road commissioner. I congratulated him on the publicity he received from the cleanup story and asked him if he wanted more.

He stammered that he didn't do it for publicity but didn't hesitate to ask what I meant. I explained about the pending project to clean up the park and how we needed police protection if we were going to do it.

"I could have called the park board," I said "but I thought you could take care of it."

I had tried to deal with the park board before and figured I would have more success going around it. Gordon would go to the mayor if he had to in order to get more publicity. I always figured he wanted to be mayor some day.

After he assured me he would look into it, I went to bed. I was sound asleep when police arrived.

I got up, let them in, and dressed while a patrolman and Andy Brown looked for the slugs. They found a hole above where I fell and a slug imbedded in the wall. Apparently the second slug had gone through the wall. They spent some time looking in the room next door without finding anything except cobwebs and a pile of old newspapers.

I invited Brown and the patrolman to Otto's for coffee, but Brown declined for both. After they left, the cat appeared. I wanted to talk so I offered it milk. While the cat lapped, I explained everything that had happened so far and asked if it had any ideas on how to advance the investigation.

It stepped back when the bowl was empty, fussed with its whiskers for awhile, and then leaped onto the desk. But it offered nothing in the way of advice, only a rumbling of contentment. I tried to take comfort in the fact that at least one of us was enjoying life.

As I was about to leave, Maggie came into the room, cheeks flushed from climbing the stairs.

"I heard you were shot. Are you all right? I didn't intend to see you again for awhile. I really don't want to get too involved. But I had to find out. Well, are you?"

"I'm all right now that the love of my life is here."

"Don't talk like that. You look okay to me. I'm going back to work. Try to stay alive."

Gordon called before I could get back in bed. He said police would be there the next morning before noon. This thing was getting out of hand. I didn't have time for this stuff, but I didn't want to spoil BJ's delight in having something to do. So I agreed to have "my" cleanup crew there the next morning and exacted a promise from Gordon that he wouldn't tell the local media anything about it until the story was published in Chicago. He gleefully promised when I mentioned Chicago.

I spent an hour looking for BJ. I found him in one of his favorite places, the park. I had my camera with me and took several "before" shots. He was delighted when I took one with him in it. After worrying about my wounded arm, he assured me he could find Little Jack, James and Lump. He started picking up debris and putting it in a pile. I warned him to leave before late afternoon when the drug pushers would take over the place.

"And remember what I told you about roaming around late at night. You might get mugged. I know you hang around some times looking for me, but you shouldn't do it late at night.

"You can always find me in the daytime. Isn't that right, BJ?"

86

He nodded.

"I try to remember what you tell me, Mister, but I forget. I did something I wasn't supposed to last night. I think it was last night."

"What?"

"I was waiting for you to come home. I just like to see you sometimes when I get tired of being by myself. I wasn't going to bother you er nothin'. I saw that little man run out of your building. It was after those big noises, the bangs."

I questioned him extensively. He thought I was angry because he had been hanging around at night when I told him not to. All he could say about the man he saw or thought he saw was that he was short, slight.

"Are you sure it was a man?"

"It must have been, Mister. He was wearing pants and a black hat."

It was a shame what had been done to Hellerman Park. The three tennis courts at one end were nothing now but weed infested slabs of cement with faded lines and broken nets.

The baseball diamond was littered with cans and bottles, and the wooden bleachers were now mostly ashes. The boards had been burned in late night fires.

There was plenty of work to do. Would it do any good? The commissioner said he had been assured police would patrol the place and keep the drug pushers away, but I had my doubts.

When I showed up the next morning about ten o'clock, the little park already looked rejuvenated. BJ, Little Jack, who seemed to be in charge, and the other two were there. So were a number of children and some parents. The children were running back and forth with anything they could find to pick up and throw on an increasing large pile. James, Lump, and an adult I didn't know were raking.

Little Jack spotted me. He came nearer and said, "Got shot just so you won't have to do nothin'. How is it?"

He seemed impressed with me. For getting shot? Maybe it was because I had been able to get police protection. Two patrol cars were parked along side the park, and four cops were making their presence known by walking around twirling their nightsticks.

From somewhere a riding lawnmower appeared, and James cornered the honor of driving it. He frowned with concentration as he guided the machine until every blade of grass was properly trimmed. There wasn't that much. Mostly, once the debris was gone, there was nothing but bare dirt. Two trees, one with a broken limb hanging almost to the ground, had survived. Several others were dead.

A city truck appeared, and many eager hands shoveled, raked, and tossed junk into the back of the vehicle. Cheers followed when the driver got back into the truck and waved to the gathering crowd. Young and old faces gleamed as they smiled and cheered. I saw tears. I took shot after shot of faces, the truck and several overall views of the park. I had a good story with art.

I managed to get BJ, Little Jack, James, and Lump together for a photo and had trouble convincing them I couldn't promise it would be in the paper.

I telephoned the story to the Chicago Times feature editor who was interested when I promised no one else had it yet. I got the negatives on the next bus for Chicago, and they had the whole package in plenty of time for the next day's morning edition.

Gordon, BJ, his three coworkers, Otto, Faustine, and a few others were impressed the next day with the story and photos. Guys and gals in the local media were unhappy. Too bad. I wondered how soon the drug pushers would take over the park again. And there were all those names, including mine, that they could blame for losing their "store," even if it was only temporary.

I talked Gordon into having one of his crews cut down the dead trees and plant new ones complete with protective wire around them. He agreed, and later I got a call from the parks commissioner wanting to know why I hadn't contacted him.

I had hoped he would call. His name is Packard, Arthur Packard, and he is a pompous ass who does nothing but grow fatter off taxpayers' money.

"I thought you probably were out of town, attending another of those meaningless, luxurious conferences you political types stage."

"Kiss my ass. You'll never get anything out of me again."

I hung up. I never got anything newsworthy out of him anyway.

CHAPTER FOURTEEN

It was time to get back to work for the guy who was paying me. I contacted Linsley Sinclair's mother again. She invited me to her house, worried over my wound when I got there, and wondered what the world was coming to.

We had oatmeal cookies dotted with fat raisins and coffee that made my taste buds demand more. It was great for the stomach but provided nothing for my investigation. She said her daughter went out the night she was murdered, probably to Charlie's where Mrs. Sinclair thought she was spending a lot of time, although Linsley wouldn't admit it. I stayed long enough to be polite, but she apparently had nothing more to tell me that would help.

I assured her I would take care of my wound, left, and went to the golf course clubhouse looking for Charlie.

The bartender talked on the phone and then said Charlie was playing cards and would be done in about an hour. I bought a soda, went outside, and sat on a verandah overlooking the first tee. So this is how the rich lived. I watched several different persons whack the little ball, some of them expertly, some about the way I would. It's one of those games that never appealed to me, although some claim there is a great deal of similarity between a good golf swing and a good arm swing in bowling.

The day was warm and pleasant. An occasional cloud drifted by in an otherwise clear blue sky. I put my feet up on a nearby chair, stretched, and went to sleep. Charlie woke me, spilling some of his drink on my face. I thought, at first, that he was drunk, but after he sat down opposite me and asked what I wanted I could see that he wasn't.

"I heard about you getting shot," he said. "Is that where?"

He pointed to the bandage partly visible under the sleeve of my summer shirt. I nodded.

"Could have been worse," he said.

"I'm trying to trace the movements of Linsley Sinclair the night she was murdered. I understand she was at your restaurant earlier that night."

"Who told you that?"

"Do you know what time she left and if she left with anyone?" I said.

"She left with Sluppleman. They asked for me, and I came in to see them. I hadn't seen Sluppleman for some time. We talked about high school, what was going on with us, and about two hours later they left. Must have been around eleven o'clock."

"Why didn't you tell me this before?"

"I didn't want to get involved. But Ruth, you know, Laura Beckert, told police Lins and Sluppleman were here so I had to admit it."

I had been hired to help clear Doctor Sluppleman of murder charges, and everything seemed to point to him being guilty. I was wondering what Sam Spade would do now when Charlie said he had to get back to his card game.

"Is there anything else you haven't told me?"

He stood and said, "I told police, and I might as well tell you. I think Sluppleman did it. He must have blown his cork. Lins mistreated him in high school, and maybe he never forgot it."

"Why kill Hubbard?"

"I don't know," Charlie said as he turned and walked away.

Back at Otto's my wound was aching again and I felt lousy. I wasn't earning my money. I was going to file a report with Sluppleman although he hadn't asked for one. All I could tell him was that everything pointed to him as the murderer.

It didn't get any better after Faustine came in, picked up a glass of beer at the bar, and joined me in the booth.

"Sluppleman had dinner at Hubbard's house the night Hubbard was killed," she said after she gulped beer and wiped froth from her top lip.

"I talked to Hubbard's wife, Mary. She said she fixed pot roast, baby carrots, and little new potatoes. She said Sluppleman and Hubbard talked about their high school days.

"Sluppleman left, according to her, about eleven. The time of both murders has been fixed at around one a.m. Why didn't Doctor Sluppleman tell us all of this?"

"Because he's guilty?"

Faustine shook her head.

"Fremont Randolph doesn't think Doctor Sluppleman is guilty. Randolph wants a meeting with us soon. He said he would call and set it up."

Faustine said, according to Mary, Hubbard went out soon after Doctor Sluppleman left. Mrs. Hubbard said her husband told her he was going to the downtown office to work.

90

"Nothing unusual, she said. He did it all the time, according to her. She used to worry about whether he was meeting another woman, but she said she had reached the point where she didn't care. I feel sorry for her."

My arm felt better and so did I. I pumped Faustine about her work in Chicago but didn't get much out of her. I also tried to get her to talk about her personal life. She changed the subject.

"Why don't we get something to eat and play some pool," she said.

I agreed, and we finished our beer, ate, and wound up in Sam's Pool Hall a few doors away from Otto's. I might have known she would be good.

She could put all kinds of English on the cue ball and play position for the next shot, for the next several shots maybe.

She drubbed me. My ego was shattered. But I had an excuse. My arm hurt. Actually it did, a little, and of course, it was awkward trying to line up a shot with a wounded arm.

When I suggested we do something else, anything else, she said, "Do you feel up to getting a bowling lesson."

Somewhere along the line she had washed all the makeup from her face, and a few freckles were visible. It occurred to me that she was pretty, big mouth and nose included. An alcohol-induced illusion, I decided.

She spent a lot of time finding a house ball that satisfied her.

"You wouldn't play pool for anything. Do you want to bet something on bowling?"

"I don't want to take your money. No matter how good you are, you are at a disadvantage with a house ball."

"It doesn't have to be money. How about a little sex, maybe? That way everybody wins."

There was something wrong with me. You'd think, as much effort as I put into making out with women, that a deal like that would be right up my alley, so to speak. But she was drunk, and I would be taking advantage of her. I could almost see Maggie smiling.

"Let's just bowl," I said.

She appeared angry. A woman scorned, etc.

So, we bowled. The rhythm of her delivery and the number of revolutions she created on the ball indicated she was good.

But I knew the lanes, and I had my own hand-fitted ball, all advantages that allowed me to defeat her easily. My right arm ached, but I managed to ignore it enough to bowl well. When we finished, my ego recovered from the drubbing on the pool table, I offered to buy her a drink. We went back to Otto's and sat in a booth in back.

"That's the fourth bottle of beer for each of you," Otto announced when I came to the bar to get two more.

"Keep counting," I said. "When we get to ten, I'm taking her home."

"If you get to ten, you better take me along. You won't be worth much."

It was getting close to midnight, and we had talked of many things, but still I knew little of Faustine's personal life.

While she was in the rest room, I decided we should be doing some detecting and began wondering how we could sneak into Hubbard Furniture's downtown store. I wanted to check Hubbard's files and see if I could find the second one on "Lins." I supposed the police had found it, but still, what if they hadn't? There might be some useful information there.

I explained all this to Faustine, who said, "Let's go see."

She claimed she had never met a building she couldn't break into and said if a hairpin wouldn't do it, some lock pics she had in her purse would.

"But we better find an unlocked window or some other way because a store would most likely have burglar alarms," she said.

"Wait a minute. I don't think this is such a good idea. I'll try to get his secretary to let me examine his files."

Faustine got up and headed for the street. I followed, demanding to know where she was going. I followed her as we walked up to the newer business district and the few blocks to the store.

The streets, with the dim street lights, seemed dark until we got to the store and stood across from it. Now the darkness disappeared. I imagined eyes, police eyes, watching our every move.

"I'm getting out of here. Come on, this is crazy."

"Go ahead, I'll do it by myself," Faustine insisted.

Before I could stop her, she was across the street and tried the front door. It was locked.

"You never know," she said.

We tried to lift a trap door on the sidewalk that led to the basement. It wouldn't budge. We went around the side of the building without finding a door or window. In back we found a large door that also was locked. I sighed with relief and urged her to join me in going back to Otto's.

"There's got to be a fire escape," she insisted and started around the other side of the building. It was darker in the space between the store and the next building. We groped our way. She held my hand while I tried to avoid tripping. She was looking up.

"There it is, see," she said, pointing.

I could see, outlined against the sky, a fire escape. But it was beyond our reach.

"You lean against the building and hoist me up. I can reach it and pull it down."

She pressed against me and raised her arms so she could lean against the building.

"Now make a sling out of your hands, and I'll step into it and then you lift."

She put one bare foot into my hands. As she straightened her leg, I felt the full weight of her. I got a facial impression of the middle of her body as it pressed against me on the way up. I staggered under the weight and moved away from the building. She was stretched across my face, part of her weight still supported by her hands extended against the building.

As I sagged to the ground, she bent over me like a soft, heavy pillow. We paused, me sitting on the ground holding my wounded arm, and her draped over my head. She struggled to get up, but I held on, convinced that our position then was better than anything we had experienced so far. She put her hands against my shoulders, and pushed free.

"We could do this if you were sober," she said.

"If I was sober, I wouldn't be here. And if you were sober, you wouldn't be here either. Let's go. Your place or mine?"

We managed to find her shoes after bumping into each other a few times. We groped hand in hand out of the darkness.

No one in sight. She headed toward her motel. I followed. We didn't talk. We were no longer holding hands. When we got to her door, she turned toward me and said, "It was fun. I'll see you tomorrow."

She unlocked the motel unit door, went inside, and closed it without further comment. She probably thought I was going to beg. I don't do that. Most of the time I don't do that. I went home and fed the cat.

CHAPTER FIFTEEN

It was ten o'clock the next morning before I got over to Otto's. I figured Faustine still would be angry. I need not have worried. She didn't show. Otto was strangely quiet and allowed me to mull over the sports pages without comment.

When he could see I was about to leave, he said, "You know, I like that Faustine. She got on my nerves at first but now... Anyway, I don't want you to hurt her."

"I'm sure she'll welcome your concern."

"No, damned you, don't tell her. All I want is for you to, well, don't treat her like you do some of the others."

"What does that mean?"

"If you don't know, forget it."

I slid off the bar stool, thanked him for his hospitality, and asked if he was Faustine's mother.

Standing across the street from Hubbard's Downtown furniture store, I recalled the night before. I walked into the space between the buildings and looked up at the fire escape. A good jump and I could probably grab it and pull it down. It had seemed so much higher when I was trying to lift Faustine. But enough reminiscing, I decided as I returned to the front and entered the store.

A male salesperson, complete with suit and tie, a friendly smile, and a "May I help you" appeared.

"I'm here to see my fiancée, Millicent," I said.

"Your fiancée, Millicent – Millicent Hiller?"

I left him standing there, his mouth partially open, and went to the back of the store and Millicent Hiller's desk. Her hair was strawberry blonde now. Her eyes were as bright as I remembered them. She informed me it would be impossible for me to go through Mister Hubbard's files.

"And besides," she said, "the police already have."

When I asked if I could see the manager, she huffed a little and indignantly contacted him. He appeared with a questioning look on his face. Miss Hiller introduced me to Loren Biggs and explained that I was investigating the murder of Mister Hubbard and wanted to see his files.

"Certainly not," Mister Biggs snorted.

"I'm surprised," I said, "that neither of you seem to be interested in finding out who killed Harold. I'll have to talk to Mary about this."

"Mary? Mrs. Hubbard? Harold's wife?"

"Yes," I said. "She is very much interested in doing anything that will help solve this murder. Shall I call her or just bring her to the store?"

We finally agreed that Biggs would watch, and that I would, if I found them, only look at any files pertaining to Linsley Sinclair. It took awhile, but I found the one I was seeking. It was filed under "Lins." There also was a file under the name "Ramsey Sinclair." I would have liked to look at that one also but Mister Biggs said no.

I sat at Hubbard's huge desk and read the "Lins" file. Millicent had been instructed to stay and watch me while Mister Biggs went back to what he said was his busy schedule. I figured Millicent Hiller probably did more work in a day than mister management did in a week.

The file contained a sort of journal written in pencil and sometimes pen. The entry on the first page was labeled "Senior Year."

It seemed, judging from the entries, that Harold Hubbard was infatuated with Linsley Sinclair and had been for a long time even though she would have nothing to do with him.

He described her regal bearing, "like a queen" and how she finally accepted him, even talked to him when they were alone sometimes, after she began dating Charlie Connor and Charlie insisted Harold come along.

Millicent provided note paper and pencil when I came to the only part of the journal that interested me. Harold described the night he, Charlie, Laura, and Linsley were in a station wagon drinking from a case of beer Charlie had obtained.

Hubbard described how he had longed to take Linsley in his arms and kiss her right there in front of the others and how they all talked loud and laughed and had a great time "until... I'm not going to put it down. It's too awful."

Until what!

The entry ended there. I searched through the following pages trying to find more information about that night, but there wasn't another word.

There were copious notes about how sad Hubbard was when Linsley went away to college, how she came back, how Charlie seemed to hate her later, and how she dated Hubbard, much to his delight, until he found out she was trying to make Charlie jealous.

I began at the beginning again and read everything. Still nothing that shed more light on the night in the station wagon with the beer.

Millicent asked if I was through and could she have the file so she could get back to work. She had to repeat the request because I was concentrating on trying to imagine four young apparently inexperienced drinkers in a station wagon and what might have happened.

"Yes," I said. "This has been a great help. Thank you."

At least I had some new ammunition to fire at Laura Beckert and Charlie. I got my car, drove to Laura's apartment building, and rang. No answer. It was about noon. I figured she might show up later or get up if she still was in bed, so I went around to the diner where Sluppleman and I had eaten. I killed an hour and returned to the apartment building.

I rang. She answered and invited me up, "Although," she said, "I have nothing more to say about those murders, those horrible murders. If you have something else to talk about come up. I'll be in the shower. The door will be open."

I sank into her soft couch and listened to the shower run. I watched the doorway just in case she presented the bare essence of her being again. She didn't. She was fully clothed, apparently ready to leave, when she came into the living room.

"Well, Mister Detective, what can I do for you today?"

She looked younger than before. Less makeup. And her eyes were no longer red and tired. Instead they were friendly and inquisitive. Apparently she had a good night's sleep.

"Did you know that Harold Hubbard kept a journal about his high school days and after?"

She was walking toward the kitchen as she attached a glittering earring. She stopped, paused, and without turning said, "No, did he?"

She turned. Her face was pale. All the color there a moment before was gone. As I looked at her without saying anything further, she said, "Well, did he?"

"Yes."

She continued on to the kitchen and returned with a cup of coffee. The color was back in her face, and her eyes were bright.

"I was wondering if you remember a night during your senior year when you and the rest of the grand quartet were drinking beer in a station wagon."

She handed me the coffee and said, "Why don't we go to the

table. I'm not going to sit on that ridiculous couch."

Her upper lip quivered slightly as she spoke. Was it nerves or just my imagination? She poured herself coffee and sat across from me. Her hand shook as she set the cup down.

"What did he say? We drank beer sometimes when we could get it. Linsley never drank much. The rest of us got silly once or twice. In a station wagon? Maybe. I'm not sure. Why?"

I told her about Hubbard's description of the night Charlie got a case of beer and how she and the rest, according to his journal, drank it. In a station wagon.

She tensed and said, "It must have been Linsley's mother's station wagon. That's the only one I can think of. What difference does it make?"

"Because of what happened. It had to be something roomy, like a station wagon."

"What did that weasel say happened?"

After explaining I couldn't reveal what Hubbard wrote because of the investigation, I said, "It looks like you were about to go out so I'll leave. Tell Charlie hello for me."

"What? Oh, yes. He promised to take me to lunch today. He should be here soon."

She spoke so quietly it was difficult to hear. She did not see me to the door. I moved my car half a block from the apartment building and waited. Charlie showed up in a white Mercedes, an older one, but still a Mercedes.

He entered the building. I waited, not sure what I planned to do when they came out. What point would there be in following them to lunch?

I waited. And waited. It gave me time to think about Maggie, about Faustine, about Laura, about everything and nothing. It seemed I had been on this case since the last time the Cubs won the Series. Well, not that long, maybe, but long.

I felt a little guilty about Maggie. Was I taking advantage of her vulnerability because she was separated from her husband? No. She started it, and if she was using me for a substitute how could that be my fault?

And what about Faustine? Was I going to become involved with her, if she would allow it? She was fun and bright and single, as far as I knew. But why should Maggie be denied the pleasure of my company just because she was married? Besides, she didn't wear a ring.

I was moving my legs and my rear end for the umpteenth time. It was like trying to find comfort in a woman's purse. Charlie came out of the building alone.

No lunch with Laura? I followed him and wound up in the parking lot of the golf course. I passed the point where Charlie parked and placed my Escort among the workers' cars. I waited a few minutes. When I entered, I spotted him at the bar staring into a mixed drink.

"Hi," I said in my usual jovial fashion. "I was hoping to find you here."

"Why?" Charlie said as he stirred his drink slowly, not looking up.

"I thought you were going to lunch with Laura?"

"Look, you've upset her with your talk about Harold's journal. She doesn't need to be reminded that two of her best friends were murdered. Why don't you leave us alone? I've got a notion to bust your face."

The bartender, who had been watching a soap opera on television, came down the bar casually, as though he hadn't just heard Charlie threaten me.

"Is there something I can do for you Mister Connor," the bartender said. I wondered if he intended to hold me while Charlie "busted my face."

Charlie waved him away.

"May I buy you another drink," I asked.

"Go to hell," Charlie said quietly.

I slid from the bar stool, smiled at the bartender, and said, "Maybe this is hell, Charlie."

I drove to the police station. The nearest I could find a parking space was two blocks away. I might as well have parked behind my office and walked from there.

Brown was out, I was informed. In his office I sat and waited. It seemed that was what I had done most of the day. There is value in waiting, however. I learned that as a reporter. Some of my best pieces came as the result of waiting, being persistent, and luck. I needed some luck on this case. How about finding the second file on Linsley Sinclair? That was luck wasn't it?

I was dozing when Brown came into the office. As I sat up with a jerk, he sat down, riffled through some papers, looked with disgust upon my lowly being, and said, "What?"

"If you go back to Hubbard's downtown store you'll find a journal in his files labeled "Lins.""

"And?"

"It's more evidence, I think. Anyway I looked at it and found it interesting."

"My people checked, why didn't they find it?"

I explained how it was filed under "Lins" instead of Sinclair, and that probably was the reason they missed it. Sometimes it's hard to be humble. I wasn't even trying.

"Mister Biggs, the store manager, wouldn't let me look at anything except that file, but there might be files on Charlie Connor and Laura Beckert. There's one on Ramsey Sinclair."

"We know. We looked at those. I'll have some pick up the other one. Thanks."

"Sure," I said. "That's why I brought it to your attention just like I'll bring anything else I find."

"Okay, Bancroft, so you're a good boy. I appreciate it. Incidentally, you were shot with a .38 revolver, the lab boys tell me. How is your arm?"

"I notice it once in awhile but it's only..."

"I know, it's only a flesh wound. Get out of here. I'll keep you informed as much as I can. Sorry about getting pissed."

"You had a right. But I'm still interested in whatever is going on out at Charlie's. I've got a right. After all, someone shot at me."

Brown suggested that if it had been one of the low lifes from out there, they probably would have killed me.

"Unless they were just trying to scare you."

I left satisfied that Brown and I were friends again and that he would pass along some inside information soon on either the murders or the restaurant or both.

As I got out of the Escort in the parking lot behind my office building, I thought of having the car washed and polished. It was just a temporary thing, forgotten by the time I passed Maggie's office. She was giving me the cold shoulder again.

I talked to the cat for awhile. It now was in and out of my office at will whether the door was locked or not. It assumed a petting position most of the time when I sat at the desk. We had worked out a system. I sat sideways to the desk so I could put my feet up on the corner and still pet the cat.

It was four o'clock. Time to go over to Otto's and have a beer. Still, I sat there petting the cat and listening to it make contentment sounds. Here was an animal that once had to scratch out a living, who knew what frightening experiences in the city jungle, and still could sit on my desk in complete contentment.

It reminded me of my life, minus the contentment. I meandered over to Otto's. I was even thinking of going to a movie. I leaned against the bar, my foot on the rail. Maybe, I decided, this for me was like petting was to the cat. I began to hum a tune I hadn't thought of in years.

"You better sit down," Otto said.

"I'm content, I think I really am for the moment, just the way I am," I replied.

"Okay, but I have to tell you, Helen is back."

I sat down.

CHAPTER SIXTEEN

Otto left to wait on a customer at the other end of the bar. Helen was back! Did I want to see her? Of course I did but, at the same time, I dreaded it. What if she was mired in the muck of her old ways again? Could I cope with that now? I became involved with her at Otto's. I had finished an assignment for the guy who willed me the detective agency and was enjoying a beer.

There was a commotion. Otto, me, and the three or four other people in the place turned and watched a young woman stagger toward the bar after she banged her way through the door.

It occurred to me that I probably was sitting on the same bar stool that I was when she fell against the bar, twirled, and landed in my arms.

After steadying her, I helped her get balanced on the stool next to mine. I ordered coffee. She mumbled something about not wanting coffee. She wanted a drink and spit out a few words I never expected to hear from an attractive woman, even if she was bombed.

She knocked the coffee off the bar and said she was going to leave. Instead, her head flopped down, making a sound like a melon dropped on the floor. She was out. It was only about seven o'clock, and I had planned to spend a couple of hours there, so I stayed. Besides, somehow I felt responsible. I couldn't leave her like that.

Otto and I agreed he didn't want her sleeping at his bar so we lugged her limp body to a back booth and stuffed her into it like a rag doll that refused to stay put. She would have slid under the booth if I hadn't been there. I managed to cross her arms on the table and placed her head there. She smelled of stale booze and perspiration.

I brought my beer to the booth and sat across from her. She mumbled, jerked convulsively, and went back to sleep. That lasted for about fifteen minutes. She started mumbling again and then shouted herself awake. She managed to lift her head and stared at me with bleary eyes.

"Keep your hands off me, you pervert. I'm not a whore. You can buy me a drink, but I'm not a whore."

I ignored her, hoping she would go back to sleep. Otto had warned me I would regret it if I befriended her. He wanted to call police and let them haul her to the drunk tank.

"You can bet she has been there before. She's not a customer of mine so what do I owe her?"

"Right," I said. "You don't owe her a thing. But she's not bothering anyone right now. We'll feed her some coffee after while, and maybe she'll be okay."

Otto growled and said, "Can that *we* stuff. If you want to nurse her back to the point where she'll want more to drink, go ahead. But leave me out of it."

A couple of hours later, she still was sleeping fitfully, waking once in awhile and making some lucid statement about drinking or perverts. Once she said something about being an actress.

Otto helped me pour her into a cab. I told him I was taking her to my apartment so she could sleep it off and clean herself up before she left. He warned me again, threw up his hands, and returned to the tavern.

He was right. It was two months of worry, constant worry about what she was doing while I was working at the newspaper. She stayed on the wagon for three days the first time. She had a one-room apartment across town and worked, when sober, as a waitress.

Once she was on my doorstep when I got home from work. Her hair was dirty and hung in strands. Her makeup streaked down her cheeks. Her blouse was torn. I could see she wasn't wearing a brassiere.

I thought of Otto's warning and knew, as I always had, that he was right. Still, I couldn't stop trying to help her. She reminded me of my mother, blue eyes, blonde hair, high cheek bones, lips shaped like a bow. She had no relatives, as far as I could learn.

My mother raised me alone from the time I was ten. My dad was killed in a car accident. I suppose she drank before, but I don't remember noticing it. After dad's death, she took a job as a waitress, we moved to a small apartment, and she drank.

I said she raised me, but, I guess I raised myself mostly. I read about alcoholism when I learned that was what was the matter with her. Once I understood, I felt sorry for her and spent four years nursing her back to sobriety. I thought that was what I was going to do with Helen. I didn't expect to fall in love with her and hate it because while I was lusting for her, I also was aware of how much she reminded me of my mother.

Otto's return brought me back to the present. I stopped remembering and asked the big question. "Was she sober?"

"I'm not sure. She was on the phone. When I told her you probably would be here about four, she said she would come by to see you. Said to tell you to be sure and wait for her."

We were silent for a few moments. An overhead fan groaned occasionally, and a fly buzzed past my ear. I still had time to leave. She didn't know where I lived now. I could escape. But I sat there. I ordered another beer and went to a booth and sat facing the door. Thinking again of how she banged her way into the place the first time I saw her. I was startled and delighted when she entered. She was wearing a suit, sky blue like her eyes. Not a wrinkle in sight. The short skirt revealed her long, slender legs. A pair of darker blue, high-heeled shoes accented the graceful elegance of her as she glided to the bar. A shoe-matching purse hung from her shoulder.

My delight in seeing her evaporated as she stood tapping her foot and waiting for Otto. I didn't hear what she said, and as Otto waited on her, she turned so I couldn't see what she ordered.

She turned again and spotted me. She came toward me with a cup of coffee in her hand. Her smile was radiant.

"Nick, I'm so glad to see you. I was afraid I would miss you. I've got to catch a plane to Chicago in an hour, and tomorrow I'm flying to Hollywood. Nick, I'm going to Hollywood. Can you believe it? I've been acting in a play at the Greenfield Theater. Someone saw me, and now I'm going to test for the other woman part in a movie romance. I'm on my way back to Chicago from St. Louis."

I knew a little about her acting career. I had followed it through the Chicago papers.

"You look wonderful. I knew you could do it. But don't lose track of reality. You still have to pass the screen test."

"Yes, I know. That's why I had to see you again. To keep my feet on the ground."

From the purse, she took a folded, wrinkled piece of typing paper and handed it to me.

"Read it to me again, please. I've read it a thousand times, especially when I was getting shaky, but I need to hear it again from you. I know the temptations I'll face if I fail the screen test."

"Helen, look at yourself. You are young, beautiful, have already established yourself as an actress in Chicago, what do you need from me?"

She took my hand. The warm feel of hers on mine sent shivers through me. It wasn't sexual. It was the kind of connection I felt with my mother after she quit drinking. She held my hand before she left to live with her sister in Arizona.

Our eyes met. There were tears in hers. Maybe mine too. She released my hand. I opened the folded paper and was about to start reading when Faustine walked in. She stopped when she noticed Helen, stood for a moment, turned, and went to the bar. She perched on a stool with her back to us. She was close enough that I was afraid she would hear as I read.

After I read the first sentence, Helen urged me to read louder so she could hear. Her "please Nick" was enough to melt any worry I had about being embarrassed that someone else would hear.

It was a thing I had written for my mother while I still was in high school. It was based upon what my mother had mumbled to herself while drinking in our apartment, stuff I had read, and my own gut feeling.

So I read:

"You know you are an alcoholic. You keep pretending you can take one drink or a few drinks and stop whenever you want to. But you know, no matter how much you rationalize, you won't stop.

"And what happens? Every time? It's like going back to a boyfriend who keeps promising you romance and love and, instead, every time, shits on you, shits in your face. WHY DON'T YOU WISE UP AND GIVE YOURSELF A CHANCE TO LIVE?

"Don't take that first drink ever again and tell your miserable 'boyfriend' to go to hell."

Reading it brought me right back to the night my mother staggered in four hours after midnight. She had been sober for a few weeks, and once again I was hoping it was permanent.

I was so angry. At her, I suppose, but even more than that, at the whole situation. I wrote the note while she slumped across from me, passed out.

Helen was talking.

"What did you say?"

She looked at me with those beautiful, clear eyes.

"I was saying that I really didn't need you to read the note to me as much as I wanted an excuse to see you. I just can't thank you enough for all you did for me.

"And such a gentleman. You never once laid a hand on me. Most of the time, especially at first when I had gone through so much vileness because of my drinking, I appreciated it.

"Later, I began to worry that I never again would be good enough for someone like you. But I've got my confidence back. I'll bet I could seduce you if I had the time."

"You did that long ago," I mumbled.

"What did you say, Nick?"

"I said I'm sure you could."

We were silent. I wondered what the future held for her and prayed – yes I guess I actually prayed – that she would be able to stay sober. I knew what a struggle it had been for my mother.

She reached across the booth and took my hand, pulling it gently toward her. She caressed it until my gaze met hers.

"Sweet man, I'm going. Just wanted you to know..."

I touched her lips with the tip of a finger before she could say more.

"I know, I know. Go knock 'em dead."

She released my hand, placed the strap of the purse over her shoulder, stood, and walked out with the same confident air she displayed when she entered.

I sat there for a few minutes looking at the hand she held. I got up and went outside to make sure she was able to get a taxi. She was gone.

CHAPTER SEVENTEEN

I returned to the booth, finished my beer and sat there, unaware of the others, deep in thought about Helen, her future, my future, should I get up and get another beer, deep stuff like that.

An amazing thing happened. Otto came to the booth, plopped a glass of beer in front of me, and said, "Here, it's on the house."

I had seen him wait on couples at a booth occasionally but never on regular customers. If you wanted something from Otto, you went to the bar. I looked at him and we both smiled sheepishly.

"She looks great, doesn't she," I said.

"She does, and so do you."

He turned and went back to the bar. Faustine slid from her stool and came over. She asked if she could join me. I expected her to want to know all about Helen, but she didn't ask. Otto probably filled her in. She looked at me. I was embarrassed.

"I thought you were pissed off at me," I said.

She shook her head, smiled, and said, "Not any more."

She had a puzzled look on her face, like she was looking at a painting she didn't understand.

"So, what's new," I asked, trying to get her to talk and stop looking at me that way.

"Oh, yes, I almost forgot to tell you. Sluppleman's lawyer wants us to meet him and Sluppleman tomorrow afternoon at the Holiday Inn to discuss what we've learned and what we're doing. He says he wants both of us to give him written reports as well."

We sat there, making small talk occasionally.

"Well, I guess I better go back to the motel room and start writing my report. I hate reports, don't you?"

I said I didn't mind them since writing was what I did often as a reporter. She said good night and left. I sat there for a few minutes, got up, waved to Otto and crossed the street.

After climbing the stairs to my office, I felt listless, melancholy. I turned on the radio and listened to a sweet and low love song. Tears formed in my eyes. It was ridiculous. I was glad no one was there.

The cat appeared, made hunger sounds, and rubbed against my legs until I got up and poured some milk. As the cat lapped milk, I talked to it about my mother, about Helen and about the case.

The cat jumped on the desk when it was finished and presented itself for petting. I put my feet up, and we listened to the music. Eventually, I went to sleep. I was rudely awakened when my feet slid off the desk and slammed onto the floor.

I turned the radio up a little so I could hear it in the other room and went to bed. When I awoke the next morning, the cat was sleeping on top of the blanket near my feet. The wound on my arm seemed to be healing properly, but the bandage was in bad shape so I changed it, with much difficulty.

After going over to Otto's for coffee and a couple of doughnuts, I came back to the office and wrote my report.

The cat, which disappeared shortly after I got up, was back reminding me I hadn't fed it. As it ate, I watched, at a loss for anything to do before the afternoon meeting. My mind drifted back to Helen. She didn't need me now, and I was glad, wasn't I?

Somehow the time passed. I did do some checking and learned Laura Beckert owned a 1995 Buick, the car Faustine and I saw her drive away after she got off work the night we were tied to the chairs.

Finally it was time to report to Fremont Randolph and Sluppleman at the Holiday Inn. Faustine was waiting for me in the lobby and directed me to a small conference room.

We sat around a polished table. Faustine poured coffee from a carafe. Randolph shuffled papers, and Sluppleman fooled with his hands, cleaning already clean fingernails with a dainty knife.

"So," Randolph said, "tell us what you know so far Faustine and Mister ... er, Bancroft."

Faustine read her report. It wasn't much, but her uncle didn't seem to mind.

As I read mine, he stopped me now and then with questions. Sluppleman looked bored until I reported how he left the motel, according to my information, at about eleven the night Linsley Sinclair was murdered.

He didn't deny it, but his boredom apparently was over.

Randolph questioned me about my source and said, "Then we can assume the police have talked to the clerk as well."

I agreed we could assume that.

"Well, Mister Bancroft, it seems you've been successful in gathering evidence against our client. Now perhaps you could concentrate on gathering evidence to clear him.

"I've been successful so far in delaying any court action on this matter, but we are running out of time. You two are going to have to do better. Find something that will throw doubt on our client's guilt. We all know he didn't commit these crimes. But we must prove it or at the very least create doubt. We are relying on you. You are cooperating with each other, aren't you?"

Faustine said we were. I nodded. Randolph looked at me with questioning eyes. Did he know I was holding something back?

He said, "We'll keep in touch."

The meeting was over. Faustine wanted to talk so we stopped at the motel snack bar on the way out. It was gleaming stainless steel and Formica with plastic booths designed to be uncomfortable.

I tried to convince her we would be able to get more if we kept digging, but I wasn't all that sure. When I told her I was headed for Otto's and my thinking booth, she said she would meet me there after she went back to her motel room to "freshen up."

At Otto's, it wasn't long before I had something new to think about. Charlie Connor came in, spotted me, and squeezed into the booth.

His face was red. He pounded one fist into the other. I waited for him to speak. I wasn't that anxious to find out what pissed him off because I suspected it had something to do with me.

"Those bastards beat her up. They think she told you stuff about their damned restaurant and what goes on there."

"Who are those bastards, and who got beat up."

"You know, those two muscles at the restaurant. They pushed Laura around. She's got a black eye and bruises on her face."

"Why does she call herself Ruth Romano?"

He smashed his fist onto the table, spilling my beer, and demanded, "What the hell does that have to do with this? It's because of her son."

"I thought it was your restaurant," I said.

He was so angry I was hoping he would tell me more. I thought he was going to punch me when he said, "It was Sinclair's restaurant, but now these crooks from Chicago have taken over. What does it matter? I want you to stop talking to Laura Beckert. They might kill her. And you, too. Stop talking to her."

He waited, apparently expecting me to promise. When I didn't, he moaned, "You're all a bunch of bastards."

I grabbed my nearly empty glass as he jarred the booth getting out. He went to the bar, ordered a shot of bourbon, downed it, paid, and left.

It was time I talked to Andy Brown again. I called the police station and assured him I would be right there. He said he was about to leave.

He was waiting at the door when I got there and ordered me to make it quick. I told him about Charlie and what he said about Laura Beckert being pushed around.

"Don't worry about it. Those punks are about through pushing anyone around for awhile. If you want that story you've been harping about, be here at eight tonight."

I wanted more information, but he held up his hand to stop me and said, "Just be here. I'm going home to supper. Don't say anything to anyone. Nothing."

I walked back toward Otto's but decided to go to my office instead. I wanted to write everything I knew about the restaurant because I suspected the place was going to be raided. I wanted to have as much information available as possible so I could call the Times and sell them the story. If there was a story.

As I was finishing my preparation report on the restaurant, Faustine tapped on the door and walked in. By then the cat was sitting on my desk, but it hopped down when she tried to pet it.

"A one-man cat apparently," she said.

"I guess. What's up?"

"You said you would meet me at Otto's. When you didn't, I came over to see if you're okay."

"I'm fine. I decided I had to get some work done. It's a report on another job. Has nothing to do with the murders. I'll be working on it for some time yet. Maybe I can get over there later."

It looked like she might stay around, but she shrugged her shoulders, gave me a questioning look, and left.

I watched television, tried to read a book, and finally it was time to go to the police station. I didn't think Faustine would have waited around this long to follow me, but still ... I ducked into a doorway and stood there for a few minutes, waiting for her to appear. She didn't.

I walked toward the bowling lanes, ducked down an alley, and wound up at the police station a few minutes before eight. As I stood on the steps leading to the station, Brown opened the window of an unmarked car and told me to get in.

"So, what's the mystery," I asked.

"For one thing, we're going to catch some politicians with their pants down," he said.

He checked his watch, leaned back in the driver's seat, and waited. He kept looking at his watch. I did the same. At exactly eight o'clock, he began driving. I was eager to ask where we were going, but I didn't want to give him the satisfaction.

"When we get there you stay in the car. Don't get in the way. Got that?"

He won. I had to ask.

"Get where?"

"I promised you, if you cooperated by staying away from Charlie's, that I'd give you a shot at the story. We are going to raid the restaurant. You'll be surprised at what we find, I hope."

"Upstairs, no doubt."

"Right, upstairs."

"I figure the place is a fancy whore house," I said.

"It is. But it's not the whores we're after. It's the customers."

Brown parked the car near a group of others where men were emerging. He pointed at me as a reminder I was to stay put. He got out, and nine men, all policemen obviously, in spite of being out of uniform, gathered and talked quietly. I rolled down the window and heard the familiar voice of State Police Captain Marvin Thorpe reminding each man where he was to be inside the restaurant.

I'd talked to Thorpe several times over the years in connection with pieces I was doing and once interviewed him for a report on state police work.

He signaled, and they went into the restaurant, one or two at a time, like a sudden flood of customers. I doubted they would fool the head goon for long, but maybe by then it would be too late.

I sat back and tried to relax. I was fighting a desire to go in and watch. Maybe I could stay back where Brown wouldn't see me and get back to the car before he did. But I had promised. I might need him in the future, so I decided to stay put.

As I composed in my head a lead to the story I planned to sell, the front door on the driver's side flew open and Tony Carbrunda, the guy who kept me from going upstairs, the guy who helped strip me and Faustine, pushed a gun in my ribs, and said, "Make a fuss, and I'll kill you."

I did not make a fuss. He looked for the keys to the car, found they were not there, and wanted to know if I had them.

"Police Detective Andy Brown has them. It's his car. Him and eight other cops will be out here any minute."

"I know that, you dumb shit. Why'd ya think I'm here? I gotta get some wheels. My damned car is in the garage for a checkup."

He poked the gun in my ribs again and pushed me out of the car. He followed, struggling to get across the seats. He kept the gun aimed at my belly after he ordered me to face him.

110

I was ordered to find an unlocked car. We prowled around, him behind me with the gun pressed against my back. Most of the cars the police came in were unlocked, but no keys were left behind.

"Keep looking, and move faster or I'll eliminate you right now," Carbrunda snarled.

We checked every car in the parking lot. A few more of them were unlocked, but none had keys in them. I was surprised he didn't try to jump start one. I didn't know how to do it, but you would think a crook like this guy would know.

After checking the last car, he herded me across the road that fronted the restaurant. We headed through a grove of trees toward the golf course. Apparently he knew about the course and thought he might find a car with keys in it there.

It was darker in the woods. He pushed me in the back with the gun. I stumbled along because of the tree roots and underbrush. The more I complained the more he pushed. It was easy for him. I was the one crashing into the undergrowth. He just followed in the openings I created.

It would be nice to think I was smart enough to flop down all of a sudden so he would fall over me, and then I would grab his gun and shoot the son of a bitch.

But, I tripped. He did fall over me, and let me tell you, the bastard weighs a ton. He struggled to his feet, still clutching the gun, and, as I got up, he hit me on the head above the left eye with the barrel.

I went down again, and as I did, I grabbed for something to keep from falling. That something turned out to be his legs. When I realized that's what I was holding I drove at him like a football tackle.

He went down on his back. The gun went off, sounding like a canon. At the same instant, there was a searing flash. He screamed that he couldn't see.

My hands pushed against his chest as I struggled to get to my feet. His hands covered his eyes. I scrambled away on my hands and knees, planning to get to my feet and run. My hand touched the gun. I crawled backward until I touched it again. Now I was brave. I stood up and shouted at Carbrunda to get up before I spilled his guts. I actually said that.

He struggled to his feet, still holding his hands to his face. I wiped blood from my forehead. It was starting to get into my eye.

"We're going back the way we came," I told him, "and if you make the wrong move, you're gone."

It sounded tough enough but, looking back, I wonder if I would have pulled the trigger. I've never shot anyone. He apparently gained at least partial sight. He stumbled and tripped once. I was a few steps behind and managed to stop before I tripped over him. My eyes had become accustomed to the dark, and I could see better than when we started.

As we entered the restaurant parking lot, a bunch of people gathered near where the police had parked their cars. I marched Carbrunda toward them. Brown emerged from the group and came toward us.

When he got near enough to recognize me, he said, "I thought I told you to stay in the car, Bancroft."

"Yeah, you did. Here take the damned gun so I can wipe my face. This is Tony Carbrunda, but I suppose you know that."

Detective Andy Brown smiled. I'd seen it happen before but not so often that it didn't grab my attention. He took the gun and motioned Carbrunda toward the group of policemen.

"You must be slipping, big man, to let this guy get the drop on you."

Brown followed Carbrunda and watched as others cuffed him, forced his head down, and pushed him into a police car. It drove away, following a loaded paddy wagon. The cops began to disperse.

My head ached, and the blood, although not flowing as fast, still seeped out from under the handkerchief I held to the wound. I sat in the car, glad to get off my feet.

"We got two state representatives, a state senator and some lesser sinners," Brown boasted as he eased his way into the driver's seat and started the car.

"I better get you to the hospital so they can patch you up. What happened? Did Carbrunda plan to use you as a hostage? How the hell did you wind up with the gun? Incidentally, it's a .38. We'll have it checked to see if it's the one used to wound your arm. They'll have to put a new bandage on your arm, too. You are a mess."

As we drove to the hospital, I answered all of his questions and didn't bother to pretend I got the gun because I was smart enough to fall on purpose. My head hurt.

He left me at the hospital and said he would have someone bring me to the police station so he could fill me in on the raid. He said they would be there in a few minutes. Ha. It took nearly half an hour for me to get a bandage on my head and another fifteen minutes to fill out papers.

I sat there stewing for another half hour until a young cop

showed up in a patrol car and drove me to the police station. I was getting more angry by the minute. I knew Brown had other things to do besides feed me information so I could file a story, but still, I brought in one of the star players, didn't I?

Finally, he emerged from his office, saw me, went back into his office, came out, and handed me a copy of a statement he had prepared for television and the press.

"This is it? This is all I get? You promised me, you bastard."

Brown smiled, again. He was having a good night.

"I'm going to overlook what you called me because of the bump on your head. I promised you just what you've got, a few hours start on the rest of the news jackals. I won't release that statement until tomorrow morning. You can tell that to whoever buys the story from you. Don't forget to tell them how you captured one of the bad guys."

I stood there reading the statement and realized it was complete enough to provide the basis for a good piece. Brown was gone and I had to get back to my office for the background I had prepared.

After failing to get a ride, I jogged the several blocks to my office. My head throbbed. I caught my breath and telephoned the state desk at the Times and began a fifteen-minute conversation that finally convinced the editor on the other end that I had a story worth buying.

He assigned a rewrite man to me, and I dictated the story complete with background, raid, names, charges to be filed, the whole bit.

I gave the guy telephone numbers and names so he could verify what I had reported. One of the names was Brown, and I hoped the guy would be able to get in touch with him because I wanted Brown's name to be in the article as many times as possible. It never hurts to stay on the good side of a news source.

When I read the story the next morning, Brown was quoted in elaborate detail on how an "investigating reporter," me, captured a Chicago mobster who tried to use the reporter as a hostage.

CHAPTER EIGHTEEN

State Representative Powell Brewster jumped at the chance to get special consideration if he cooperated with police. He told how he and several other politicians "were trapped" into doing the bidding of the Chicago people who took over the restaurant. It started innocent enough, he said. They were invited to the restaurant for free meals and use of a conference room whenever they wished.

Gradually, over a period of several months, they were offered free overnight stays on the second floor and free use of prostitutes. Those who were foolish enough to take the bait soon were shown photographs of themselves in unclothed and embarrassing situations.

The whole operation had only progressed, according to Brewster, to the point of forcing the suckers to buy furniture at outlandish prices. And, of course, they bought from Harold Hubbard, who was connected to Ramsey Sinclair, who was connected to the Chicago group.

I learned later that Sinclair tried to stop me from investigating further into the death of his daughter because the Chicago people insisted. They didn't want me snooping around their restaurant.

The Times bought another piece from me that explained all of this. I now had a good Chicago connection. The cleanup stuff and these pieces gave me an edge on anything I might come up with in the future.

It was late afternoon before I got to Otto's bar. Faustine was there. She was furious because I hadn't contacted her.

"Randolph is angry. He wants you to get in touch with him right away. He's been after me all day to find you."

"What's his problem?" I said as I ordered a beer.

Otto served me a cup of coffee, and when I pushed it away, he said, "It isn't four o'clock yet."

"Randolph is pissed because he thinks you have been spending all of the time Sluppleman is paying for on this restaurant story," Faustine said. "You better call him."

I did. He was angry, all right, but I calmed him down when I

114

assured him I just sort of fell into the restaurant story while I was investigating the murders.

"I expect to have some information in the next few days that will clear Sluppleman and convict the murderer," I said.

After I hung up, I wished I hadn't promised so much. Could I deliver?

It was fun, up to a point, telling Faustine and Otto what a hero I was. They wanted every detail of my encounter with Tony Carbrunda. Finally, Faustine stopped the recitation with the question, "Where do we stand on this murder investigation?

Where, indeed? As we went to a booth and discussed it, I got a call from Brown. He said the .38 special Tony Carbrunda had was the same one used to wound my arm.

"But get this," Brown said. "About twenty years ago, the gun was registered to Robert Beckert, Laura Beckert's dad, you know, the former mayor. Tony won't say where he got it."

"How about letting me talk to him?"

"Check with me tomorrow, maybe I can set up an interview. How's your head? Incidentally, Charlie Connor is out on bail."

"I'll survive," I said. I returned to the booth and Faustine.

"Well?" she asked.

"Charlie Connor is out on bail. He's only a small player in the restaurant thing, but he probably is more than that in the murders. Tomorrow, why don't you give him a call? See if he will talk. Tell him you are part of a team of Chicago investigators here to gather information to clear Doctor Sluppleman. He probably won't talk to you, but I want to put more pressure on him. Ask him about his son."

"His son? Is he married? Of course he could have a son anyway, but what son? Tell me more so I know what I'm talking about."

I convinced her she knew enough and that it was only to get his reaction. Did he have a son? It was just a shot. We agreed to meet the next day for lunch.

I walked Faustine to her motel. I told her I had a headache, which I did, as we stood at her door, each waiting for the other to make a move. I said good night and left. At my office, I found that if I sat very still with my head cocked at a certain angle, it didn't ache as much. The cat sat for awhile, waiting for me to pet it. It gave up and spread out on the desk. We listened to radio music.

I nodded off. My feet slid off the desk and thumped me awake when they hit the floor. It was an uncomfortable shock to my head. It throbbed for awhile as I lay in bed trying to put the pieces of the murders puzzle together. When I stopped flopping around trying to find the most comfortable position, the cat took its place at my feet, and I went to sleep.

My head no longer ached when I awoke the next morning. I had slept eight hours. The radio newsman still was chattering about the restaurant raid and was reporting the details I had sent to the Times the day before.

Brown managed to get permission for me to interview Carbrunda. I didn't expect him to give me any information I could use to sell another piece, but I did hope he would tell me something about the gun. I tried to convince him he would be doing himself a favor by revealing where he got it. He wasn't talking.

"The only reason I agreed to talk to you, sucker, is because I wanted to get out of the damned cell. This interview is over."

"We know the gun originally was registered to Robert Beckert, Laura, er, Ruth Romano's father. Why don't you admit you got it from her? The gun has been used in a murder."

"What murder?"

I had his attention now.

It was a lie, of sorts. The gun may have been used in a murder, but if it was, I didn't know about it.

"Well," I said, "if you want to allow the record to show the gun is yours, so be it."

He seemed close to talking. But he didn't. The code of silence is strong among his type. I headed back to my office. I hadn't seen Maggie Atley for a couple of days and was wondering if I was back on her "ignore him" list. I didn't see her when I went by her office.

The phone was ringing when I reached the third floor. I kicked a letter on my way to answering it. The guy on the phone was from the Times. He wanted to check on some details for a follow-up story on the restaurant raid. He said they were sending one of their reporters down to report on any court developments. In other words, forget the story from now on, we'll take care of it.

After I hung up, I went back and got the letter. It was from Maggie. In it she said she quit her job and went back to her husband.

She wrote, "Thanks for the memories," and signed it "You know who."

I sat and tried to understand how I felt. Not much of anything, I decided, although I pretended to hate being used as a sex toy.

As I stroked the cat, which now appeared most every time I sat down at the desk, I decided Maggie was a nice person, and I wished her happiness.

"Thanks for the memories," I said to the empty room.

Faustine met me for lunch at the diner across the street from the police station. She was excited.

"I thought you were going to get me killed, having me ask Charlie Connor about his son. He went berserk. `What are you talking about,' he shouted at me."

"That's a real threat to your life, all right," I said.

"You should have seen his face. Anyway, I think you are on to something. I don't know what it means, but the way he acted, he has a son. So why don't you tell me what this is all about?"

"It's about who killed Linsley Sinclair and Harold Hubbard. I'll explain it to you later. I want you to go with me to see Laura Beckert. You pretend you are from child welfare. You don't have to be specific, just pretend."

We were lucky. Laura was in and invited us up to her apartment.

"I suppose you're happy now," were her first words.

"I'm out of a job. I know you had something to do with the police closing the restaurant. I read the stories."

"Yeah, maybe," I said, "but we are here about your son. Miss Smith here is from child welfare."

The color drained from Laura's face.

"What are you talking about?" she whispered as she collapsed onto the soft couch.

She looked small and defeated as she put her hands to her face and added, "You have no right to do this. What are you talking about?"

"Charlie told us," Faustine said.

"Yes," I added, "Charlie and Doctor Sluppleman."

"Doctor Sluppleman wouldn't tell you. When I told him about it, he promised he wouldn't tell anyone. What kind of a doctor would tell you? You're lying."

I pulled up a chair and pushed my face close to hers.

"Let me tell you how it is. You shot at me with your father's gun. Either you wanted to kill me or scare me because you thought I was getting too close. Carbrunda somehow got it and wacked me with it. If you don't go with us to the police station and confess to everything I'm going to call your dad in Florida and maybe even talk to your son.

"And if Doctor Sluppleman goes to trial for murders you committed, all of the details of how you became pregnant, how you became a whore at the restaurant, all of it will be splashed over television, the radio, in the papers. The news media will have a ball. They'll camp outside your dad's house and hound your son, the kid who doesn't even know his mother is alive. Is that what you want?"

She sobbed for several minutes. Faustine sank into the couch and put an arm around Laura's shoulders.

"It was Linsley's fault. She put that stuff, I guess you know, GHB, the rape drug they call it, in my beer. Then she and Harold Hubbard watched while she egged Charlie on until he raped me. She thought it was funny, knowing how I loved Charlie. I guess she wanted to show him I was a slut.

"Just last year, when she was jealous because I was working at the restaurant and around Charlie all the time, she told me in her superior way what happened in that damned station wagon. I didn't even know. All I knew when it became obvious I was pregnant, was that my father was going to throw me out if I didn't go away to have the baby and leave it with him and his sister. When his sister died, he kept my boy. He wanted his grandson, but he didn't want me. I visit once a year and pretend to be my own baby's aunt."

She slumped even further into the folds of the couch and sobbed again.

"Why did you kill Hubbard?" I asked.

She hesitated, as if trying to remember.

"Because the bastard sat there in the station wagon and watched. Linsley told me. He kept saying it was wrong, according to Linsley, but he never did a thing about it."

"Why didn't you kill Charlie?"

"Because I love him," she wailed. "He, he never would have done it, he told me, if it hadn't been for Linsley."

"How did you get Linsley and Hubbard to sit still while you pushed a needle into them?"

"I put some of that horrid stuff in their drinks. It knocked them out just like it did me. Then I shot them full of it with a needle."

We took her to the police station. I called from Laura's apartment to make sure Brown would be there. He met us with a stenographer, a tape recorder, the whole bit.

When it was over, Faustine walked back to my office with me and tried to get the cat to sit still so she could pet it. It moved away every time she got near.

I called Doctor Sluppleman and was told he would call back between patients. Faustine and I talked about things in general and the murders in particular.

Finally, she said, "Well, if there's nothing else I'll go back to the motel, pack, and return to Chicago."

It was deadly quiet after she left. Doctor Sluppleman eventually called. He was delighted, of course, but said he felt sorry for Laura. He said he would help her plead insanity.

He didn't seem particularly upset about how Laura tried to frame him for the murders by putting Linsley's body at the football stadium – the scene of Sluppleman's high school humiliation – or the fact that she planted evidence against him at both scenes.

"She's sick," was all he said when I asked him about it.

Even his promise of a sizable bonus didn't raise my spirits.

It was time to go over to Otto's for a beer and more of his stimulating conversation. Instead, I turned on the radio, put my feet on the desk, and talked to the cat.

It had worked its haughty way into my life. It didn't demand anything except a little food and drink. It never added anything to the conversation, but, on the other hand, it never argued.

So I talked. I explained to it, and to myself, how I felt incomplete, as though something was left undone. What had I forgotten? I had an urge to talk to Andy Brown, but I didn't dare call him at home. As he had said many times, he would arrest me.

I went over to Otto's and had a beer, went for a walk, and finally went up the hill to a movie. Back at home, I didn't sleep well and was up early the next morning, anxiously waiting for the time to pass so I could talk to Andy.

When he finally got to his office, I was there waiting for him.

"I don't think she did it," I said.

He left the office, came back with a bunch of files, put them on his desk, and gently rubbed his head.

"Who?"

"I don't think Laura Beckert is a murderer. I think she is protecting someone, probably Charlie, or at least she thinks she is protecting him. I don't know that he did it either. I don't know anything except that I feel..."

"What you're feeling is normal. We all have doubts when we nail someone for murder. How can anyone be absolutely sure? What the hell do you want me to do about it? She did confess."

"Suppose, just suppose that Doctor Sluppleman, he's smart, we all know that, just suppose he set this whole thing up so we would put pressure on her, and she would confess to protect her kid or Charlie or both."

"I've thought of that. But why would he kill Linsley Sinclair after all these years? Why would he kill Hubbard? And how could he set it up so Laura Beckert would confess? How could he be sure she would? What about the gun? How did he get it? Did he shoot at you? Lots of questions. No answers."

He agreed to fix it so I could talk to Laura Beckert that afternoon. She already was insisting she didn't want an attorney.

She looked ten years older than she had the last time I saw her. She sat at the table in the jail interview room. The room was small and bare with two chairs and a table. A police woman stood guard outside the door.

The skin under Laura's eyes was as dark as night. Her hair hung limp around the loose skin of her face. She sat like a sack, showing no interest in her surroundings.

"Why did you confess to two murders you did not commit?"

Her head jerked up. She looked at me for the first time, her eyes alert.

"What?"

I repeated the question.

"Did Charlie tell you to do this? I don't care what he says, I did it. I just want to get the trial over with. You promised me you wouldn't involve my son. You promised."

She wiped away tears, braced herself, and repeated quietly, "You promised."

I assured her I had no intention of involving her son, no matter what happened, but I didn't want her to take the blame for two murders if she wasn't guilty.

"I'm responsible for you being accused, and I'm having doubts. I think you are trying to protect Charlie as well as your son. Why would Charlie want to kill Linsley and Hubbard?"

She raised herself from the chair by pushing against the table with her hands, shuffled to the door, and tapped on it. The interview was over.

I slumped on a bench outside the jail and felt as depressed as Laura appeared.

It must have been at least an hour later when BJ sat down beside me. I was rehashing every detail I knew about the case and didn't want him to interrupt my musings.

"I'm busy BJ. Why don't you go look for some cans or something."

He was holding a pair of thick eyeglasses, glasses that were too small for his face. He held them up to his eyes and looked through them at me. The frames were black.

"Things look funny. Your eyes look big, like big marbles. Your nose looks funny. It hurts if I look through 'em too long."

He wasn't going away unless I demanded it. He would be hurt.

His life had improved considerably since he got hooked up with Little Jack and the other two. Little Jack parleyed the publicity they received from cleaning up the park into a cleaning business. I talked him into hiring BJ after he admitted BJ was a willing worker as long as someone told him what to do.

BJ started singing a tune I couldn't quit place and looked at me with those damned glasses. It was annoying. How can a man think when an overgrown child is staring at him?

"Put those glasses away, please. You'll ruin your eyes. Where did you get them anyway?"

"That day I found the lady who lost her clothes. The lady who died. You know. At the football field. They were under her. She was kind of sitting on them."

I bent over and put my face in my hands. Why had I been so blind? Why hadn't I asked him where he got the glasses when he showed them the first time?

"Are you sick, Mister?"

I stood and put my hands on his shoulders.

"Give me those glasses and come with me. We're going to see Detective Brown. Come on."

He hung back.

"I didn't do nothin', honest. I don't want to go in there. They put me in a cell once with awful people."

"It's okay. I won't let anyone arrest you. It's just that we have important evidence in those glasses. Brown will thank you. You can trust me."

He hesitated, handed me the glasses, and said, "Don't tell him I took them. I found them, honest."

Brown put the glasses in a plastic bag and reassured BJ he wasn't going to be arrested.

"I'll turn these over to the lab guys. If they belonged to Sluppleman we won't have too much trouble proving it, and he'll have a lot of explaining to do. Thanks Mister Broadway John. You have been a great help."

BJ beamed as we left the station even though his questions indicated he didn't understand how he had been a "great help."

The lab guys and police detective work proved the glasses belonged to Sluppleman. He had them replaced by his optometrist three days after Linsley Sinclair was killed. In the meantime, he wore a spare pair.

He was arrested and charged with the murder of Linsley Sinclair after Laura Beckert testified that she gave the gun to Sluppleman when he warned her it was a dangerous thing for her to have. She said she was surprised later to find it in her purse. And still later, when Carbrunda saw it, he took it away from her.

I talked to Laura Beckert after she was released.

"What I don't understand is why Sluppleman wanted to frame you?"

"He wanted me to sleep with him. I was his patient. I told him everything about the rape, about how Linsley had thrown the whole thing in my face. I told him everything, and he wanted to comfort me with sex, his sex. He became violently angry when I refused.

"It was horrible. He screamed at me. I screamed at him. I told him if he wanted sex he should go see Linsley. I sneered at him about how she would love that."

"Why did he kill Hubbard?"

"I don't know for sure. I told Harold about my sessions with Sluppleman. He was always kind to me. He even dated me once in awhile, but he still was interested in Linsley. And, of course, I was interested in Charlie. Maybe Harold threatened Doctor Sluppleman. I know when I threatened to tell Harold about Sluppleman's advances he became very angry. Poor Harold. I should have been nicer to him. We all should have."

I told Brown what Laura Beckert told me, and he used the information when questioning Sluppleman. Brown and the other police who had been interrogating Sluppleman off and on for two days were about to give up when the doctor cracked.

Sluppleman confessed and pleaded insanity after Brown threatened to question all of the doctor's female patients.

Back at my office, when it was over, I put my feet on the desk and petted the cat, my cat. And thought about Maggie.

Finis

Dear Reader,

I hope you enjoy the story *Murder by the Book*. I would love to hear from you. Email me at BancroftMysteries@gmail.com or follow the wild and crazy adventures on:

www.BancroftMysteries.com/

https://www.linkedin.com/in/BancroftMysteries/

https://www.instagram.com/bancroftmysteries/

https://www.facebook.com/BancroftMysteries/

https://twitter.com/BancroftMyster1

All the Best, Martie Liter Ogborn

Made in the USA
Monee, IL
14 July 2020